Advance praise for STAR-CROSSED

"*Star-Crossed* delighted me! Barbara Dee has a light touch and a pitch-perfect middle school voice. This book will have you laughing and groaning in sympathy with crush-addled Mattie and eagerly turning pages. Mattie and her classmates charmed me with their kindness, their humor, their uncertainty, their devotion to one another and to—Shakespeare! Barbara masterfully sprinkles the Bard's words over the narration and stirs the troubles of Romeo and Juliet into the plot. And those Shakespearean insults! Be sure to read *Star-Crossed* or you'll miss out." —Gail Carson Levine, author of *Ella Enchanted*

"Barbara Dee's *Star-Crossed* is a love story, a rallying cry for girl power, and a Shakespeare lover's dream come true. When I finished reading, I had a huge smile on my face and a lightness in my heart." —Nora Raleigh Baskin, author of *Nine, Ten: A September 11 Story*

"*Star-Crossed* takes the drama, humor, friendships, misunderstandings, and romance of *Romeo and Juliet* and transforms them perfectly to the middle school stage. One word about this honest, heartfelt middle-grade novel for the theater geek in each of us? 'Encore!'" —Donna Gephart, author of *Lily and Dunkin*

"*Star-Crossed* by Barbara Dee cleverly draws from *Romeo and Juliet*, providing readers with an insightful introduction to Shakespeare while exploring the complexities of young love. Readers will root for this relationship." —Ami Polonsky, author of *Gracefully Grayson*

STAR-CROSSED

BARBARA DEE

ALADDIN

NEW YORK LONDON TORONTO SYDNEY NEW DELHI

ALADDIN
An imprint of Simon & Schuster Children's Publishing Division
1230 Avenue of the Americas, New York, New York 10020
First Aladdin paperback edition March 2018
Text copyright © 2017 by Barbara Dee
Cover illustration copyright © 2018 by Margaret Kimball
Also available in an Aladdin hardcover edition.
All rights reserved, including the right of reproduction in whole or in part in any form.
ALADDIN and related logo are registered trademarks of Simon & Schuster, Inc.
For information about special discounts for bulk purchases, please contact
Simon & Schuster Special Sales at 1-866-506-1949 or business@simonandschuster.com.
The Simon & Schuster Speakers Bureau can bring authors to your live event.
For more information or to book an event contact the Simon & Schuster Speakers Bureau
at 1-866-248-3049 or visit our website at www.simonspeakers.com.
Cover designed by Nina Simoneaux
Interior designed by Mike Rosamilia
The text of this book was set in Minion Pro.
Manufactured in the United States of America 0719 OFF
10 9 8 7 6 5 4
The Library of Congress has cataloged the hardcover edition as follows:
Names: Dee, Barbara, author.
Title: Star-crossed / Barbara Dee.
Description: New York : Aladdin, 2017. | Summary: When Mattie is cast as Romeo
in an eighth-grade play, she is confused to find herself increasingly attracted to Gemma,
a new classmate who is playing Juliet.
Identifiers: LCCN 2016029743 | ISBN 9781481478489 (hardcover) |
ISBN 9781481478502 (eBook) | ISBN 9781481478496 (pbk)
Subjects: | CYAC: Theater—Fiction. | Middle schools—Fiction. | Schools—Fiction. |
Sexual orientation—Fiction. | Family life—Fiction. |
BISAC: JUVENILE FICTION / Social Issues / New Experience. | JUVENILE
FICTION / Social Issues / Friendship. | JUVENILE FICTION / Performing Arts / General.
Classification: LCC PZ7.D35867 St 2017 | DDC [Fic]—dc23
LC record available at https://lccn.loc.gov/2016029743

For all my former students, even the ones
who thought they didn't like Shakespeare

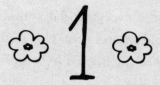

1

"In fair Verona, where we lay our scene."
—*Romeo and Juliet*, Prologue 2

It wasn't about me, I knew. But still.

I hadn't been invited to Willow's Halloween party, and I was okay with it. Unlike a lot of my classmates, I didn't plan my schedule around her parties, which were usually sweaty and overcrowded, the sort of thing where you spent the whole time shouting over music you'd never listen to on your own. She'd always invited me to her Halloween parties before, and I'd always gone, mostly because my two best friends, Tessa Pollock and Lucy Yang, were going, and the three of us always stuck together. Everyone knew this, even Willow, who never paid us much attention. The weird thing was how she'd invited Lucy (even though she never hung out with Willow) and Tessa (even though Willow pretty much hated her). But not me.

"Don't feel bad, Mattie," Lucy urged me. She looked worried. Lucy was always fussing over this sort of stuff, trying to make sure everyone felt comfortable. The idea that she was invited when I wasn't . . . well, I could tell she felt terrible. "I heard she invited only half the class, so I'm sure it wasn't personal."

"How could it not be personal?" Tessa demanded. "Willow decides who's invited and who's not. What could be more personal than *that*?"

"You guys, I'm fine," I insisted. But still, I tried to think if I'd offended Willow lately, if maybe I'd forgotten to congratulate her on scoring a goal or something. Willow was the type of person who expected face-to-face compliments, not just cheers.

Tessa snorted. "Of course you're not *fine*, Mattie. How could anyone be *fine* about being left out of the biggest party all year?"

We were at Verona's, this new fro-yo place in town where you could design your own sundaes. I was having chocolate fudge with chocolate chips and crushed brownies, Lucy was having strawberry with a bunch of fruit on top, and Tessa was having vanilla drowned in almost every topping available—gummies, marshmallows, peanut butter cups, hot fudge, strawberry syrup, coconut. It looked like a small volcano had erupted in her cup, trapping gummy bears in lava. Like a yogurt Pompeii or something.

"Well, Mattie, if you're not going, neither am I," Lucy said.

"What?" I don't know why this surprised me, because it was typical Lucy. "That's really sweet, but it wouldn't be fair. I mean, to you."

"Are you joking? Why would I do something that wasn't fair to *you*?"

"Listen, we're *all* going. Including Mattie," Tessa declared, waving her spoon for emphasis.

I took an enormous bite of my creation. "Well, aside from the fact that Willow obviously doesn't want me there, it's supposed to be a costume party, right? And I'm not a costumey sort of person."

"How can you say that?" Lucy protested. "Your costumes are always so original, Mattie. That year you went as the Sorting Hat—"

"Yeah. People just thought I was a witch."

"Okay, but last year, when you went as Matilda—"

I groaned at the memory. Last year, I'd thought: *Okay, my name is Matilda; how much more obvious could it be? Besides, who hasn't read* Matilda? So I wore my half-sister Cara's old school uniform and my brother Mason's tie, and I made my hair all crazy with spray. Liam Harrison, the coolest boy in the grade (at least, according to him), asked if I was Eloise. You know, the bratty little girl at that hotel. Clearly, I was the worst at costumes.

"I'm the worst at costumes," I told my friends.

"Maybe you're overthinking it," Tessa said. "You don't *always* have to do a book thing, do you? You could just wear a really cool mask."

"But I don't own a mask. Even a non-cool one."

She poked two holes in her napkin and held it over my face. "Voilà: mask. And the thing about wearing a costume, Mattie? *No one will know it's you.*" She stage-whispered the last part, cupping her hands over her mouth.

"Yeah, maybe," I said. "If I totally cover myself, including my head. And if I disguise my voice. But I don't know, the idea of sneaking into Willow's party—" I shook my head.

"Mattie, come on," Lucy cut in. "You can't spend Halloween sitting home by yourself; it's bad luck, or bad karma. Bad something." She ate a raspberry. "Oh, and by the way," she added, "not that it matters, but I heard Elijah's going."

I poked a brownie chunk with my spoon. "Yeah? Well, woohoo."

"Okay, so what did I miss?" Tessa had been away all last weekend at a theater camp reunion, and was still catching up on the news. "What happened with Elijah?"

"Nothing," I told her. "I saw him at the library on Sunday, so I said hello. It was like, *Hey, how was your weekend, wanna hear about mine?* He didn't even answer."

"Whoa," Tessa said. "*Literally* didn't?"

"Yep. Totally ignored me."

"Maybe he wasn't ignoring you; maybe he just didn't hear," Lucy suggested.

I raised my eyebrows at her. "In a quiet library? When I was talking exactly as loud as this?"

"Maybe he had earbuds in?"

"Lucy, he was just sitting in the graphic novel section reading old Batman comics. No earbuds, no anything. I checked."

Tessa licked some fro-yo off her spoon. "You know, I hate to say this, Mattie, but in my opinion Elijah's a stuck-up dirtbag."

"You're probably right. The stupid thing is, I think I still like him."

"That *is* stupid," Tessa agreed. "Why *do* you like him?"

I sighed. Because how do you answer that kind of question? It's like explaining why you think a joke is funny, or why a song stays in your head. Or why you like chocolate fudge frozen yogurt, or the color blue. You just like what you like. Like *who* you like. Even if the person acts like a stuck-up dirtbag sometimes.

Besides, liking Elijah was just *what I did*. What I'd done since the start of seventh grade last year, when I suddenly realized that I kept staring at him. He wasn't just cute, with his wavy dark hair and his big brown eyes—he was really smart, especially about words. He always raised his hand in English and said non-obvious things. I could tell our teacher, Mr. Torres, appreciated his comments. And how many eighth-grade boys spent summer vacation at the town library? Only Elijah.

I mean, really, considering *me*, it made perfect sense for me to have him as my crush. For an entire year, I scribbled his name in the back of my math binder and tried to think up words that rhymed with Elijah (*beside ya?*) while he read Batman comics or whatever.

Because the thing was, who else was I supposed to like?

But it was hard to say this without sounding slightly loser-ish. Or like a person who enjoyed feeling sorry for herself. Which I didn't.

"Earth to Mattie," Tessa said. "Come in, spacegirl."

"Yeah, sorry. I was just thinking." I stirred my fro-yo counterclockwise, then ate a spoonful of soggy chocolate chips. "I guess I like Elijah's eyebrows. And the way he laughs."

Tessa snorted. "Okay, well, that explains everything."

"Mattie, listen to me," Lucy said, reaching across the

table to pat my shoulder. "Go to Willow's party, wear a costume, take a really good look at Elijah. See how he acts if he doesn't know it's you. It'll be a test: If you still think he's worth spending the entire year crushing on, go ahead. But maybe you'll decide he *isn't* worth it. And maybe you'll notice someone else."

"Yeah? Like who?" By then, we'd noticed everyone in middle school. There was nobody left to notice.

"I don't know," Lucy admitted. "I just think you should keep your eyes open."

Right then, Charlotte Pangel and Isabel Guzman walked into Verona's. They were two of Willow Kaplan's sidekicks, always playing on Willow's teams, or cheering for her in the stands. Seriously, it was strange that they were here without her, because they tagged after Willow all over town. Charlotte and Isabel were the kind of girls who were always whispering to each other; whatever they were saying, it was probably something you'd rather not hear.

I poked Lucy's elbow. "Come on, let's go."

"Why?" Tessa challenged me. "I haven't finished eating."

"Just take it with you," Lucy said.

"But I *like* it here. I like these *chairs*. Don't you think these chairs are really comfy?" Tessa sat back in hers, kicking out her skinny legs as if she were sunning herself by a pool. She scooped up a spoonful of fro-yo lava and beamed at us.

Lucy and I exchanged glances. I could tell she wanted to leave as much as I did, but neither of us trusted Tessa enough to leave her behind. The thing about Tessa was, sometimes her Off switch malfunctioned. Especially around people who didn't appreciate her coolness.

So the three of us sat there, not budging, while Charlotte and Isabel helped themselves to yogurt and toppings, paid the lady at the counter, who was possibly Verona, then took seats at a table opposite us. Lucy and I pantomimed eating, even though by then there was nothing left in our paper cups.

Charlotte and Isabel whispered. The radio was playing some Mom-era song, and Possibly Verona was humming along as she sprayed and wiped the counter.

Finally, Charlotte slapped down her spoon. "Okay, that is just. So. Rude."

Tessa blinked at her. "I'm sorry?"

"Right, Tessa. Like you don't know."

"I really don't, Charlotte. Why don't you tell me?"

"The way you keep staring at us," Isabel said. "It's kind of creepy, actually."

Tessa raised her eyebrows. "You think I'm staring at *you*? Why would I even *want* to?"

"Who knows?" Charlotte said, smirking. "Maybe you're wondering what it's like not to be ugly."

Tessa paled. Considering she was naturally fair-skinned, with wispy blond hair and light blue eyes, pale on her looked kind of alarming.

But then it was like something clicked inside her, and she practically leaped out of her chair. "*I'm* ugly? *You're* like a toad; ugly and venomous. Thy face is not worth sunburning."

Uh-oh, I thought. Because I'd seen this before: When Tessa got too angry to think up words, she quoted lines from plays. Often it got on people's nerves.

"'Thy'?" Charlotte hooted. "'*Thy*'?"

"Tessa, come on, we need to leave," I said, grabbing her arm.

She pulled away from me, avoiding my eyes. "It's Shakespeare," she informed Charlotte. "It means 'your': *Your* face is not worth sunburning."

"I know what 'thy' means, you moron. I meant, who *talks* like that?"

Tessa did a fancy bow. "I do."

Isabel rolled her eyes. "Yeah, Tessa, and we all love hearing it."

"Okay, guys," Lucy said, stepping in front of Charlotte. "Can we all please . . . ?"

Tessa ignored her. "At least I *have* something to show off. But you, Charlotte, are just Willow's little shadow. You can't think one single thought for yourself. 'Thou hast no more brain than I have in mine elbows.'"

"There she goes again," Isabel told Charlotte. "'Mine elbows.'"

"Oh, is Shakespeare hard for you?" Tessa asked sympathetically. "Allow me to translate. 'Mine' means 'my'; 'elbows' means 'elbows.'"

The door opened. In walked Willow. As soon as she entered the shop, you could tell she smelled a fight. "What's going on?" she asked in a sharp, accusing voice.

"Nothing," I said quickly. "Charlotte and Tessa were just arguing. But it's over now, right?" I glared at Tessa.

"Really?" Willow narrowed her eyes at me. "Well, it doesn't *look* over. It doesn't *feel* over."

"Because it's not," Charlotte said. "Tessa just basically called me stupid."

"Huh. Did she? The thing is, Tessa, if you're being nasty to my *friend*—"

Tessa's cheeks turned pink. "I'm just defending myself, Willow! Am I supposed to *stand* here and allow your little lapdog—"

"Okay, so now you're calling me a *dog*?" Charlotte's eyes popped.

"No," Tessa said. "Although, actually, 'I do wish thou *wert* a dog, that I might love thee something.'"

"*What?*"

"Should I translate, Charlotte? 'Thee' means—"

"STOP," Possibly Verona shouted. She was in front of us now, her hands on her hips. "If you girls can't have a pleasant, *quiet* conversation without name-calling, you aren't welcome here."

"But she started it," Charlotte protested, pointing at Tessa.

"That's not true," I said loudly. Lucy frowned at me.

"I don't care *who* started *anything*," Verona snapped. "It's my shop, and I can't have fighting in here, period. Now why don't you girls take your fro-yos and come back when you can act decently, like well-behaved young women."

She walked over to the door and held it open for us. It occurred to me that I'd never been kicked out of anywhere before—and I hadn't done anything to deserve it. Although in a way, I wished I had. I mean, I sort of just felt like a spectator.

All six of us filed out of Verona's. Tessa was the last to exit, and as she did, she did another fancy bow, doing a complicated hand gesture that ended with her tipping an imaginary hat.

"Fairest lady, I humbly take my leave," said Tessa.

"Yeah, right," growled Definitely Verona.

"Be rul'd by me: forget to think of her."
"O, teach me how I should forget to think!"
—*Romeo and Juliet*, I.i.228–229

By then it was almost suppertime, so without discussing it—without talking at all, really—we found ourselves heading home. Tessa's house was closest, and we were almost on her block when Lucy finally broke the uncomfortable silence.

"Okay, Tessa," she said. "So, can you explain what that was all about?"

Tessa sighed. "I know, I know, you guys. I screwed up."

"Yeah, you did. You totally overreacted in there! All that quoting Shakespeare—"

"I know! It was wasted on those Willow-ettes, anyway. All they hear is 'thine' and 'thou,' and their teeny little brains freeze up." She pretended to stiffen.

I couldn't help grinning. "I really liked the line about sunburning."

Lucy gave me a look like, *Way to help, Mattie.*

But I didn't care. "I thought all those quotes were pretty great, actually. How do you know them?"

"Theater camp," Tessa said. "Our director, Juno, had a poster with all these hilarious Shakespearean insults, and my friend Henry and I memorized a bunch: 'I'll beat thee, but I should infect my hands,' 'I do wish thou wert a dog, that I might love thee something,' 'Vile worm, thou wast o'erlook'd even in thy birth.' Although my favorite is definitely 'mad mustachio purple-hued malt-worm.'"

I burst out laughing. "What does that even mean?"

"No idea. But it's just so horrible, isn't it? The whole summer, Henry and I kept calling each other that: *Stop stealing my cookie, you mad mustachio purple-hued malt-worm!*" She sighed. "I swear, Mattie, Shakespeare is the best! He's so good it's like he came from outer space. Wouldn't it be awesome if we did a Shakespeare for the eighth-grade play?"

Lucy frowned. "Hey, guys. Can we please not change the subject?"

"Sorry," Tessa said. "What *was* the subject?"

"How you picked a fight just now. At Verona's."

"But I didn't! I was just sitting there, enjoying the comfy chairs, and all of a sudden Charlotte goes—"

"Tessa, it doesn't matter," Lucy scolded. "You responded

to her. *Over*responded. Look, the point is: We go to school with these people. We can't be fighting with them all the time, okay? And Willow's party is tomorrow night."

"Hey," I said as we arrived at Tessa's corner. "Maybe what happened at Verona's is a sign that we shouldn't go to this party. I mean, really, if we don't even *like* each other—"

"Then we should *definitely* go," Tessa finished.

"But why?"

"Like Lucy said, we're all going to school together, so we *have* to get along. Somehow." Tessa rolled her eyes. "And anyway, they need to see that they can't keep us out."

"But of course they can," I argued. "It's Willow's party; she can invite whoever she wants. Or *not* invite, like me."

"Mattie, you have to stop saying that, all right? You're going! Just start planning your costume. Text me if you're stuck." Tessa blew kisses. "Ta-ta, *mes amis*. Till we meet again."

We watched her walk to her doorstep, turn and wave like a Hollywood starlet at a movie premiere, then pivot and go inside.

Lucy exhaled. "Mattie, you *have* to come to that party. I refuse to watch her all by myself."

"Ah," I said. "So you mean we're Tessa-sitting. I thought you wanted me there so I could notice someone else. Besides Elijah, I mean."

"Yeah, that, too. Absolutely that. Both."

We began walking to Lucy's house, which was four blocks from mine. Lucy seemed weirdly quiet, and she was twirling her ponytail, which was usually a sign that she was thinking hard about something. I wanted to ask her about it, but I knew her well enough to wait. She'd let me know when she was ready.

All of a sudden, then, she was.

"Mat, can I tell you something?" she blurted.

"Of course," I said.

"Your mom called me yesterday. She said she's worried about you."

"She did? Why?"

"She said you seemed a little out of it lately. She asked if I knew what was going on."

"With me? What did you tell her?"

"Nothing. I mean, nothing about Elijah. I just said that eighth grade is hard, it's our last year of middle school, all that kind of stuff."

"Okay, good," I said. "Thanks."

Lucy looked at me. Her black eyes were full of concern. "It *is* the whole Elijah thing, right? Nothing else?"

"Why? Do I seem weird to you?"

She thought about it. "No. Just a little spacey, maybe."

"But I'm always spacey."

"Okay, spacier than usual."

I kicked some dried brown leaves as we walked. "Yeah, it's really about Elijah. I don't know, Lucy. Nothing I do makes a difference. He just ignores me."

"Well, maybe he's wrong for you," Lucy said gently. "Anyway, at the party you'll see how he acts when you're in disguise. You'll see the real Elijah, the one everybody else sees. And then you'll decide if it's time to forget him."

Lucy was a great friend, but sometimes she made too much sense. It was like her brain organized things into pro-and-con lists, or flowcharts, or PowerPoint presentations. Everything went from A to B to C, sometimes with little subheadings, and always with a conclusion. She'd never get a crush on a hopeless boy who ignored her. She was too logical for that.

But I had to admit she had a good idea with this party. Because maybe Elijah would show up in a cheesy costume, maybe as a Smurf or a seventies disco guy, or, I don't know, a Teenage Mutant Ninja Turtle. And I'd take one look at him, and *ping*. My crush would just pop, like a giant soap bubble.

Which would be kind of nice, I had to admit.

Although if that happens, then what?

3

"How long is't now since last yourself
and I were in a mask?"
—*Romeo and Juliet*, I.v. 34–35

You might think that after what Lucy told me about my mom calling, I raced home to have a tantrum.

I mean, I knew that I had every right to burst into her office and shout something like, *Mom, if you were really worried about me, why didn't you ask ME if I'm okay, instead of going to Lucy behind my back?*

But I didn't, because there was no point. My mom saved her messy, emotional scenes for my big sister, Cara. With me, everything was a calm conversation about concrete nouns.

For example, this one, from just this morning:

Her: *Mattie, I'm going to a client meeting this afternoon.* (She's an architect.) *Supper's in the fridge; if I'm running late, can you heat it up for you and the boys?* ("The boys" are my brothers.)

Me: *Sure.*

Her (kissing my cheek): *You need a haircut.*

Me: *Maybe just the bangs. I like it long.*

Her: *It's six inches longer than it was at your last cut. I'll schedule a salon appointment for tomorrow morning.*

Me: *Not too early, okay? I want to sleep.*

Her: *You're sleeping too much lately, Mattie. You shouldn't sleep more than nine hours, you know. I read an article.*

Me (smiling at lame joke): *Well, maybe I need more than nine hours. Because my hair is growing.*

Her (not smiling at lame joke): *Set your alarm for eight a.m., and don't stay up late. Love you, honey. Bye.*

I'm not complaining. She wasn't a Crazy Mom, like Tessa's, who was always ranting about politics and food additives, or a Germaphobe Mom, like Lucy's, who squirted you with hand sanitizer every time you walked in the door. My mom worked hard, never missed parent-teacher conferences or band concerts, made decent food, helped me with my homework (well, she did when I was younger), and drove me places. I was really grateful for all that stuff, believe me. But I just couldn't *talk* to her—not about feelings topics. Because the few times I tried, I could see the flashing lights going off in her brain: *Oh no, is Mattie turning difficult now, just like Cara did at this age?*

Truthfully, it didn't surprise me that she'd called Lucy to ask how I was. Lately, I'd been answering Mom's questions with a shrug or a joke—and she knew I told Lucy everything. Plus, Lucy always sounded so sane and logical. Mom probably thought the two of them spoke the same language.

"FREEZE!" shouted my brother Kayden. He was seven; Mason was eight and a half, and they were both obsessed with *Star Wars*. Their bunk bed was the Millennium Falcon, their rug was a TIE fighter, and their backpacks were BB-8 (Kayden) and the Death Star (Mason). That day they both were wearing Stormtrooper outfits, running around the house with lightsabers, chasing Jedi, or whatever.

"I'm not playing," I informed them. "Where's Mom?"

"In her office," Mason replied. "You are beaten, rebel. It is useless to resist!"

"I said I'm not playing, Mason!"

"Rebel, speak when you are spoken to!"

Sometimes their games drove me insane.

"I'M REALLY NOT PLAYING," I shouted. "Can't you hear? Doesn't that mask have ear holes?"

"Yeah, of course it does; you don't have to shout," Mason said in a hurt voice. He took off his mask and showed me. "Be careful with it, Mattie. The plastic's not as good as the Darth Vader one."

Oh, right, I thought. *My brothers have a Darth Vader costume.*

The complete thing, head to toe, with a mask that had a built-in-device-thingy that gave you that wheezing sound and made your voice sound deep and scary. And it was kids' size extra large, because all the other sizes were out of stock.

I'd never worn a store-bought costume, or even a movie-themed one. But I was sick of people not getting who I was. The party was tomorrow; I didn't have time to come up with something original. Plus, the most important thing this time was being in disguise. *Sounding* in disguise.

"Hey, guys," I said, changing my tone to Nice Big Sister. "I need to ask you both a huge, huge favor. Can you lend me the Darth Vader costume?"

"It's not a costume," Kayden snapped.

"It's not? What is it, then?"

"He thinks it's real," Mason told me.

"It *is* real," Kayden yelled. "It's a real Darth Vader suit!"

Mason rolled his eyes.

I smiled sweetly. "Yes, and it's so cool, Kayden. That's why I need it for this Halloween party I'm going to."

"It won't fit you, Mattie," Mason said disgustedly. "You're too tall."

"Can I please just try it on?"

"But what if *we* need it?" Kayden yelled.

"I'll give it right back, I swear. I'm only going to borrow it for tomorrow night. You can have it back on Sunday morning."

"Um," Kayden said. He looked at the ceiling and tapped his foot.

"Kayden, fine. I'll be Princess Leia for an hour. *Then* can I try on the Darth Vader suit? And borrow it for the party?"

Kayden whispered something to Mason, who grabbed his mask from me and slipped it over his head again.

"As you wish, rebel swine," Mason sneered.

The Darth Vader costume was perfect. A little tight in the crotch, a little short in the pants—but if I wore black boots, no one would notice. My long hair had to be crammed inside the helmet, but I would be getting a trim tomorrow morning, so that would help. The costume came with a lightsaber, of course. And the best thing about it, the breathing device transformed my voice into a not-bad Vader imitation.

Which I practiced over and over in front of my bedroom mirror. "I've been waiting for you, Obi-Wan. We meet again at last."

Also, the Vader breathing thing: "*WHEEZE.* You underestimate the Power of the Dark Side. *WHEEZE.*"

A couple of times that night, Tessa and Lucy texted to ask if I needed help coming up with a costume. I told them I was "all set," and that I wanted to surprise them. I also told them I'd meet them at the party, because I figured that if the three of us arrived together, everyone would instantly realize Darth Vader was me.

And being discovered? That was the one thing I couldn't risk.

"You have dancing shoes/With nimble soles;
I have a soul of lead/So stakes me to
the ground I cannot move."
—*Romeo and Juliet*, I.iv.14–16

On Saturday night, Mom drove me right to the Kaplans'
front door, which was decorated with a giant cobweb
spelling WELCOME. I hadn't mentioned to her that I wasn't,
in fact, welcome; it wasn't the kind of information I'd
been sharing with her lately. And anyway, what would
have been the point? She'd just tell me I shouldn't go, and
I knew that already.

"Pick you up at ten," she said, as I got out of the car.

"How about nine thirty?" Darth Vader whispered.

"Really?" Mom looked surprised. "Well, sure, Mattie,
if you want. Call me if you change your mind."

I watched her drive off. Then I Vader-marched into
the house and downstairs to the basement, which was
where Willow had her parties. Right away I spotted Tessa

flirting with Liam Harrison, who'd come dressed as Thor.

Uh-oh, I thought.

Liam was the unanimous vote getter for Cutest Boy. He was nice enough, I guess, but conceited; I couldn't figure out what Tessa saw in him, other than the extreme cuteness. Oh, and the fact that Willow made no secret about liking him. But maybe those two things were enough for Tessa, who could be really competitive. Fortunately, Lucy (Tinker Bell), was standing nearby, keeping an eye on her while chatting with Keisha Bromley (A jellyfish? A squid? Some sort of mutant combination?). And what was Tessa supposed to be, anyway? She was in black, with black envelopes stuck randomly all over her body.

Okay, got it: *blackmail*.

I almost guffawed. But, of course, Darth Vader never guffaws, so I turned it into a choky cough.

Suddenly, Lucy looked right at me. Then Tessa must have said something funny, and the four of them—Lucy, Tessa, Liam, and Keisha—started laughing. That was when I realized they had no idea who I was. And it felt a little creepy—because Lucy and Tessa were closer to me than anyone else on the planet, closer than my family, almost—and here they were, seeing me but not *knowing* me. I almost ran over to them and pulled off the mask and yelled, *Hey, it's me, guys; aren't you surprised?* But, of course, not being recognized was the whole point of this costume. And anyway, I'd come here to see Elijah.

I left the room and wandered around a bit, finally spotting Elijah in the corner of the basement, where the Kaplans kept their old stereo stuff. He was standing by himself, checking his phone, and he was wearing a suit and tie. *Weird costume,* I thought. Maybe he was supposed to be a senator. Or an undertaker.

"So we meet again," I boomed. "The circle is complete."

He looked up at me and grinned. "Hey, cool. Ryan, right? Wait—no, it's Ajay. Or Jake."

"Your limited imagination arouses pity, rebel scum."

Elijah laughed. *He really does have a great laugh,* I couldn't help thinking. "Dude, that's so awesome. You sound just like Vader."

"Thank you. I am glad your ears are functioning well today."

"My ears?"

"Never mind. I see you are wearing a suit and tie."

He shrugged. "Yeah, I couldn't think of a costume. So I'm Alfred."

"Who?"

"You know. From *Batman*?"

"Ah, yes. The butler. Of course."

"I know it's stupid. You don't need to rub it in, Jake."

"I'm not—"

"Forget it, okay?" He sighed. "I don't know why I even came. I hate big parties. All these people we never hang out with at school."

I wheezed. "Some of the girls look pretty good, though, right? In their costumes?"

"Yeah, I guess? I hadn't noticed." Elijah's dark eyebrows rose hopefully. "You want to get out of here? Get a pizza, play some Xbox, or something?"

"Me? Now? I can't. I mean, I would, but I told my mom—"

"Hey, you're not Jake." Elijah got up close to my face, so close I could smell pizza on his breath. "Okay, who *are* you?"

"I am your father," I said quickly. "So there's pizza? Where?"

"Exercise room. But you'll have to take off your mask to eat." All of a sudden, he grabbed the edges of my helmet, as if he wanted to yank it off. "It's Ajay, right?"

"Unhand me, rebel swine," I thundered. "You don't know the power of the Dark Side."

I jerked backward and turned away from him, swishing my cape. As I did this move, it occurred to me that I didn't remember if Darth Vader actually did any cape swishing, but what was the point of having a black cape if you didn't use it for emphasis?

Then I marched away in purposeful Vader steps. What had I just accomplished? Yes, I'd proven that Elijah's ears worked fine, which meant that when he "hadn't heard" me in the library, he was just being a dirtbag. On the other hand, he seemed kind of sweet just now—awkward about costumes, awkward about the party. We had more in common than I'd even realized.

Although what did it mean that he "hadn't noticed" any of the girls at the party? Was that a good sign, or a bad one? I desperately needed to talk to Lucy. Except now I couldn't find her. Or Tessa, either, for that matter. Where were they?

I searched the crowd of kids I'd known for the last thirteen years, barely any different under makeup and masks. Besides Tessa, a few girls had made their own costumes: Willow (Queen of Hearts), Charlotte and Isabel (a pair of dice), Keisha the jellyfish squid. Most of the other girls were wearing costumes to make themselves look cute—Wonder Woman, Rey, Supergirl. But besides Liam (Thor), Nolan Pike (Rubik's cube), Bennett Park (Captain America), and Elijah, the majority of boys had just thrown on football jerseys. Or drawn on their faces with Sharpies, messed up their shirts with ketchup and jelly, and staggered around like zombies.

Why had I tried so hard to be clever, with all my book characters? Tessa was right: I'd definitely overthought the whole costume thing. All I'd needed was this Vader mask and cape, and I could have avoided humiliation for the last few Halloweens. For a smart girl, I could really be dumb when it came to certain topics.

"Hey, Darth Vader," Willow said, doing a stuck-up Queen of Hearts smile as she walked over to greet me. She'd used white makeup on her face; her lips and cheeks were maraschino cherry red. "Nice costume."

"It is not a costume," I thundered.

She laughed. "Of course not. Say a line from *Star Wars*."

"Your thoughts betray you. Your feelings are strong. Especially for . . . sister. So, you have a twin sister."

"Ha-ha! That's great! Say something else!"

By then I was running out of Vader-isms, so I went for the obvious. "The Force is strong with this one."

Charlotte, Isabel, Keisha, and a few other kids walked over.

Isabel was popping candy corn into her mouth. "Who's Darth Vader?"

"I think it's Elijah," Charlotte said.

"No, Elijah's wearing his bar mitzvah suit." Isabel giggled.

"It is not his bar mitzvah suit," I boomed. "Elijah is Alfred from *Batman*."

"Yeah, he would be," Charlotte said. She squinted at me. "It's Jake, then, right?"

"Negative," I said.

Willow poked my shoulder with her scepter. "All right, Darth Vader. As your queen, I command you: Reveal your true identity! This is my party, and I demand to know!"

Under the mask, I could feel sweat dripping down my neck. "I find your lack of faith disturbing. Now, if you will excuse me, I take my leave. The Emperor awaits."

I did the cape swish again and walked away fast. Fortunately, there was a bathroom in Willow's basement. I ducked inside, locked the door, and took off the mask. *Oxygen. Yay.* Then I splashed some cold water on my sweaty face.

A minute later, someone banged on the door. Hard. And then four more times. And then kicked it.

I was about to protest—and remembered the voice-changer, just in time. Pulling on the mask, I roared: "Stand back! I now approach!"

I unlocked the door. It was Ajay Vehta, an obnoxious

boy with pug doggy eyes who probably trash-talked his own grandma. He had pizza smears down the front of his football jersey, which meant he'd either come as a zombie or was just a disgusting eater. Knowing him, probably both.

"Sorry," he muttered. "I thought it was somebody else in there."

"Mad mustachio purple-hued malt-worm," I said.

"What?"

"The bathroom is yours, space junk."

He scowled as he shut the door behind him.

I checked my phone again; now it was eight fifteen. That meant I'd be stuck here for another hour and fifteen minutes. Seventy-five minutes of swishing my cape and running away from people who wanted to know who I was. I'd already had the conversation with Elijah, so there didn't seem to be much point in hanging around. But if I called Mom to pick me up now, she'd ask what had happened, and where were Tessa and Lucy, and shouldn't we carpool? Because we always did.

I walked past the stereo corner. Someone had turned up the music really loud, and now I could see Tessa hopping around, her arms flailing. Liam was dancing too—not *with* Tessa, exactly, but she was definitely part of a girl circle surrounding him. Lucy was dancing with Bennett Park; she didn't appear to still be on Tessa duty, but maybe acting like she was having fun was part of her surveillance technique. Anyway, it was fun to watch her; all her years of ballet and tap had made Lucy an incredible dancer.

Too bad I can't join them, I thought. And what was I supposed to do for more than an hour, if I couldn't dance, couldn't eat pizza, couldn't even talk to people? Maybe Ajay was out of the bathroom by now. If he was, I could lock myself in there until 9:29. If only I'd brought a book with me.

I sighed. The voice-changer wheezed.

Then I thought: *What if I snuck upstairs to the kitchen and found a straw?* At least I'd be able to sip some water through my mask. Willow's parents had firm rules for her parties—they'd come downstairs every ten or fifteen minutes to check on us, and we weren't allowed upstairs for any reason—but I'd be quick. It was really kind of an emergency situation: With all the sweating, I was desperately thirsty. And Willow's parents were a pretty big deal in our town; they wouldn't want negative publicity (*Party Girl Banned From Kitchen Perishes from Mask-Induced Dehydration*).

I waited for a superloud song to make my move, then tiptoed upstairs, once almost bashing the banister with my lightsaber. The Kaplans' huge white kitchen was empty, except for someone getting ice cubes from the freezer.

It was a girl.

5

> "O, she doth teach the torches to burn bright!
> It seems she hangs upon the cheek of night
> As a rich jewel."
> —*Romeo and Juliet*, I.v.46–48

She turned when she heard my boots. Gemma Braithwaite, who for some reason wasn't in costume.

"Oh," I said.

She grinned. "Hullo. It's Darth Vader, isn't it? Ace costume."

"Uh, thanks," I said. Then I wheezed.

Okay. Now I'm going to say something that may sound a little weird: I'm a pretty girl. My hair is long, thick, and a nice color (medium brown with blond highlights); my eyes are hazel; my nose is straight. My skin is zitless; I tan in the summer. I'm tall, but not crazy tall, and clothes fit decently on my body. So yes, pretty, by normal girl standards.

But there's me-pretty, and there's Gemma-pretty.

Gemma-pretty was more like storybook-princess-pretty, if the princess got regular exercise. She had shiny chestnut-brown hair that she wore in a messy braid over one shoulder, large brown eyes with feathery eyelashes, a heart-shaped face, naturally red lips. Gemma played goalie on the girls' soccer team, so obviously she was strong and quick, but she didn't dress in a *Look at me, I'm so athletic* sort of way, like how Willow did. Often, Gemma's clothes were in clashing patterns that made her seem chic and European. I'd heard she was from London, living in town with her dad since last spring. And I'd heard her speaking with a posh English accent, although she didn't seem to be a snob; she said Britishy things like *Sod off* and *bollocks*, and her laughter was rowdy.

But that was all I knew about her. Not only because she wasn't in my classes, but also because as soon as she showed up in town, Willow and her friends swooped in on her. Swarmed her in the lunchroom, on the bus, at recess. Sometimes I spotted Gemma's shiny chestnut hair in the middle of a crowd, but it was never a crowd I wanted to join, or that would have welcomed me, if I'd tried. Gemma Braithwaite wasn't just a sporty, popular girl; she was a prize Willow's team had won, and they'd made it clear they wouldn't be sharing.

So it was extremely weird that here she was, all by herself, sneaking ice cubes.

And now it was my turn to say something. "Why aren't you in a costume?"

She winced. "Didn't realize that I should wear one."

"You didn't? But it's Halloween."

"Yes, but we don't celebrate it in the UK. Not the way you do in the States." She went to the sink, adding water to her glass of ice cubes. "So of course tonight I look like a complete scruff, which is why I've been hiding in the kitchen."

"We're actually not allowed up here," I said.

She smiled. "Yes, I know. If we were, it would be stupid to hide here, wouldn't it?"

I wanted to confess that I was hiding too. But Gemma was friends with Willow; it would've been insane to trust her with my secret.

Instead, I asked if she knew where they kept the straws.

"Straws?" Her mouth made a small O.

"To drink with," I explained. "Because of my mask."

She peered at my face. "Yes, drinking must be difficult. Hang on." She opened a small drawer to the left of the sink and started to rummage. "I've been doing a little snooping, but don't tell, please. They keep all sorts of fascinating things—ooh, here we are."

She held up a straw in a paper wrapper. "Shall we have a duel?"

"Excuse me?"

"I challenge you. Trusty straw versus deadly lightsaber. En garde!"

She lunged at me, slashing the air with the straw. I pressed a button on the lightsaber. Nothing happened, so I pressed again, then a third time.

"Dang," I muttered.

She lunged at me again, poking my stomach with the straw. It tickled. "*Dang?* What sort of a word is 'dang'?"

"American, you uppity British invader."

"Uppity? How dare you call me uppity." *Poke.*

"Snooty. Snobby. Stuck-up. Condescending."

"Those are fighting words, Imperial fiend!" Now she poked me in the armpit.

It was then that my weapon glowed a sort of hazy pink, buzzing like a wounded mosquito before fading out completely.

"*Dang*," Gemma said, grinning. "The Dark Side needs new batteries, I see. Well, cheers." She handed me the straw.

"Thanks." I grabbed a glass from the drying rack, filled it with water, ripped the paper off the straw, and sipped. The whole time I drank, I felt her eyes on my face. On my mask, I mean.

And then, without thinking, I un-Velcroed the black

cape from my shoulders. "Here, why don't you take this?" I said. "You can use it as your costume. It's kind of all-purpose."

Gemma looked horrified. "Oh, but I couldn't! It's your *cape*."

"It's not mine; I just borrowed it. And you can borrow it for tonight. My costume's fine without it."

"Are you sure?" Gemma tied the ends around her shoulders like a shawl and twirled. "Oh, but it's brilliant! I love it! It's my Cloak of Visibility!"

She threw her arms around me in a hug. "Thank you, Darth Vader! Even though you were vanquished in our duel, I'm forever in your debt."

"You are most welcome, Princess Gemma," I said.

Over her shoulder, I could see Willow's small black labradoodle, Pixel, scampering toward us. Probably the swordplay had sounded like dog fun to him; he was barking enthusiastically, as if he wanted to be included.

"Be quiet," I begged him, as I pulled away from Gemma. "We're not playing with you." But he just kept barking.

"Give him the straw," Gemma suggested.

"Are you nuts? Dogs don't drink—"

She giggled. "No, no, to chew on. Or carry. Whatever dogs do with sticks."

I placed the straw at his feet. His barking got even louder. Also now he was growling and showing teeth.

"I think he may be frightened of your costume," Gemma said. "It *is* rather alarming. You could take it off, you know."

"Actually, I can't."

"Why not? You mean it's stuck on? I could help—"

"No! Not stuck."

"What, then?"

Suddenly, there were running footsteps. Willow, the Queen of Hearts, was racing into the kitchen, followed by Isabel and Charlotte, the pair of dice.

"Pixel?" Willow called. "Where are you? In the kitchen? You know you're not supposed to—*Oh*," she said, finally noticing Gemma and me.

"Hullo, Willow," Gemma said, smiling calmly. "Charlotte and Isabel, what brilliant costumes. You're a pair of dice?"

"Yeah," Isabel said. "We can't sit down, but otherwise—"

"*Excuse* me," Willow interrupted. She picked up Pixel, who immediately started licking the white makeup off her face. "You know, you guys shouldn't be in here. My parents have a very strict rule about party guests upstairs."

"We're *so* sorry, Willow," Gemma said. "But it's all

entirely my fault. I came upstairs because I stupidly showed up tonight uncostumed, but Darth"—she gestured toward me—"has just now gallantly come to my rescue. Look!" She twirled again, and the cape billowed around her.

Willow returned Pixel to the floor. "He gave you his cape? Yeah, that was very nice. Whoever he is." She narrowed her eyes at me, the way she had at Verona's.

And before I could jerk backward, before I could lift my hands to stop her, or zap her with my dying lightsaber, or simply flee down the stairs, she lunged at me, yanking off the mask.

So there I was. Unmasked.

Sweaty head. Matted hair. Red face.

Charlotte and Isabel began to giggle nervously.

Gemma's eyes widened. "Oh," she said.

"Oh. My. God," Willow declared, loud enough for everyone to hear, upstairs and downstairs, even over the blaring music. "Omigod. I do *not* believe it! Everyone, you have to see this! Guess who's Darth Vader. *Mattie!*"

"My only love, sprung from my only hate!/Too early
seen unknown, and known too late!"
—*Romeo and Juliet*, I.v.140–141

I can't tell you exactly what happened after that, because
my brain spontaneously combusted.

But I do know that somehow I managed an apology
(although not an explanation), fled downstairs, made it
outside onto the front lawn, and phoned my mom from
behind the shrubbery. Tessa and Lucy ran out the door
after me—Tessa shouting, "What? She took off your mask?
That's so *aggressive*!" while Lucy was patting my back and
making soothing noises and reminding me to breathe.

"It doesn't matter," she kept saying. "It's not so bad.
Breathe, Mattie. Who cares what Willow thinks. Or what
she says. Try really hard not to overreact, okay? Take
another deep breath. . . ."

But the combination of the heat from the Vader costume

and the humiliation upstairs tumbled together with the realization that I'd have to face Willow, if not Gemma, in school on Monday. That's when I vomited. Not a massive amount, but what there was landed on Willow's mini-pumpkins.

"Oopsy," Tessa said. "Mattie, why don't we take a little stroll down the street?"

"We'll help you walk," Lucy said.

"I can walk just fine," I muttered.

"I can't believe *you* were Darth Vader," Tessa said, grinning. "Where did you get the costume?"

"Where do you think? Little brothers."

"But why didn't you tell us?" Lucy asked.

I groaned. "To surprise you. And so you wouldn't give me away."

"You think we can't keep a secret?" Tessa said.

"No. I was just scared you'd look at me a certain way, or I'd look at you, and people would realize who I was. It was stupid of me. Sorry."

Finally, my mom drove up to the corner of Willow's street and spotted the three of us.

"What happened?" she asked immediately, as soon as she saw my face.

"Nothing," I said, wiping my nose with Vader's glove. "Do you have a tissue?"

She opened the glove compartment. "Here. Don't say 'nothing.' I can see *something* happened."

"You should just tell her, Mattie," Lucy said. "Okay?"

I looked at Lucy in horror.

"Or *I* could, if that would be easier. You want me to?"

"Tell me what?" Mom demanded. "*What happened?*"

"Go ahead, tell her," I mumbled. Whatever Lucy would say, it wouldn't be the whole story, but at that point it would be a better version than anything I could come up with.

Lucy patted my arm. "Mrs. Monaghan, Mattie has a crush on someone, but he hasn't been very nice to her—"

"He's been a total malt-worm," Tessa said. "Truth be told."

"—so she came to the party to give him a sort of test. Which he failed, didn't he?"

I shrugged. I could barely remember. "I guess."

"You guess?" Tessa demanded. "You *guess*?"

"Anyhow," Lucy continued, "Mattie needed him not to recognize her tonight, which is why she wore the Darth Vader costume. But someone at the party took off her mask, and now she feels embarrassed. And mad."

Nice job, I wanted to say. Lucy had told Mom a sensible story, tactfully omitting the bit about my not being invited in the first place, and getting unmasked by the hostess, of all people.

Not to mention the whole kitchen scene with Gemma Braithwaite, which, of course, Lucy didn't even know about.

Although if she did, what would she say about it? *Mattie was embarrassed in front of a new girl from England who'd probably assumed she was a boy?*

"Well, Mattie, that does sound awful," Mom said. "We could go out for some fro-yo to cheer you up?"

Tessa, Lucy, and I exchanged looks. Probably we were still banished from Verona's; even if we weren't, I didn't want to risk Verona telling Mom about yesterday's fight. Plus, the thought of eating fro-yo—especially watching Tessa with her molten lava creations—was a little sick-making so soon after barfing on Willow's lawn.

"Lucy and Tessa need to go to Tessa's house to finish eating Halloween candy," I said, wiping my nose. "They promised Tessa's mom. Otherwise, she'll eat it all herself."

"Huh," Mom said. "That's surprising. Tessa, I thought your mom was into nutrition."

"Oh, she is," Tessa said. "But I guess everyone has a private Dark Side, right?" She winked at me as we arrived at her house. "Thanks for the ride, Mrs. Monaghan. Mattie, we'll talk tomorrow. Parting is such sweet sorrow!"

She blew a kiss and then my friends got out of the car.

* * *

As soon as Mom and I pulled into our driveway, all I wanted was to get out of the Darth Vader suit, wash my hair, and crawl into bed. Mom, of course, wanted to have a whole conversation first—Who was this crush? Did she know him? Did she know his parents? What was this "test" all about? Et cetera. I answered as briefly as I could, giving her just enough information to satisfy her curiosity.

Then I took a steaming-hot shower for twenty minutes, letting the water pound on my scalp as a sort of punishment. How was it possible to have messed up so horribly? It was bad enough being unmasked as a party crasher, earning the scorn of Willow and the Willow-ettes; but now Elijah certainly knew I was Darth Vader, which meant he may have figured out why I'd been talking to him.

As for Gemma—the whole thing was just excruciating. Because the more I thought about it, the more I was convinced she'd been sort of flirting with me, assuming that the gallant kid underneath the Darth Vader costume was an *actual boy*. Of course, I couldn't have told her who I was; and I'd never lied, or pretended to *be* a boy, so it wasn't my fault if she'd made that assumption. Besides, it was obvious that the "Vader voice" wasn't really how I spoke. She couldn't have possibly thought that's how I sounded, could she?

And if she did—well, it didn't matter. I'd probably never talk to her again, anyway.

Although the thing was, *she went to my school*. Even if we didn't have any other conversations, I'd run into her somewhere or other. It was inevitable. No way that wasn't going to be awkward.

"Awkward"—what an awkward word. It sounded like the cry of a giant scraggly bird. *AWK. WARD. AWK. WARD.*

I blow-dried my hair, brushed my teeth, and then hid myself under my covers.

7

"The orchard walls are high
and hard to climb."
—*Romeo and Juliet*, II.ii.63

Sunday morning I awoke to my little brother Kayden screaming.

"Whaa—Kayden? Why are you in my room?" I croaked, my throat still parched from the night before.

He pointed to my desk chair, where I'd draped the Darth Vader costume so that it could air out. "Where's his cape?"

"What?" I asked, sitting up.

"His cape. Darth Vader's *cape!*"

"Oh, shoot."

"Mattie, you *lost* it?"

"No, no. I just left it behind. At the party."

"*You left his cape behind at the party?*"

"Yes, Kayden, I did. Don't scream. I'll get it back this morning."

"*You'll get it back this morning?*"

"And stop repeating. Yes, I will, I swear. Don't worry, okay?"

He burst into tears.

Dang. Now I *would* have to talk to Gemma, but under the circumstances, I had no choice.

As soon as I got my brother to stop crying, I threw on some clothes, brushed my teeth and hair, gulped down some OJ, and looked up *Braithwaite, Gemma* in the school directory. She and her dad lived on the opposite side of town in one of those ugly pink apartment buildings near the train station. *I probably should call over there first, to be sure she's home,* I thought, but then I'd have to have *two* conversations with her: one on the phone, explaining the situation, and one when I went to her apartment to get the cape. Better to just walk over there and be done with this whole thing. As fast as possible.

"Hey, how was the party last night?" asked my dad. He was in his Sunday neon green bicycling clothes, which always looked so dorky I had to turn away.

"Fine," I said, slamming the directory shut.

"That's your full report?"

"Yeah. It was . . . you know. A party."

"Thanks for the in-depth analysis." Dad tied his

sneakers. "Hey, isn't it early for you to be dressed on a weekend? Are you going somewhere?"

"Just to a friend's."

"Boy or girl?" He smiled mischievously.

Oh, great. Mom had told him about Elijah.

"Girl," I said. "I just left something at the party last night. I'll be right back."

"Take your phone. Mom's out shopping, and she'll want to know your whereabouts."

"Aye, aye, Captain," I said, saluting.

He gave me a look. But I'd only saluted and called him "captain" because he'd said "whereabouts." By now, Dad should have realized that I noticed words.

The morning was chilly, so I grabbed my fleece jacket and started walking toward the train station. On my phone were three texts—two from Tessa (*you ok? you looked baaad last nite! call me!* and *Why haven't you called, you canker blossom? if you dont call by noon, I'm coming over!!*), one from Lucy (*Hey, are you awake yet? I've been worried about you*). I wanted to answer, but I hated texting while walking—and, to be honest, I didn't feel like sharing the Gemma business with them yet. Besides, if I got to Gemma's apartment, took the cape, said, *You're welcome*, when she said, *Thank you*, and kept on moving, I could be back in my bedroom in an hour. Then I could talk to my friends in privacy.

By the time I reached Gemma's building, Mom had called (*Feeling better? Want me to buy you anything at the grocery store?*), Tessa had texted again (*Where art thou?*), and Lucy had left me a voice mail (*Mattie? Why aren't you answering?*). I put all of them on hold in my mind as I hit the small black button next to the name BRAITHWAITE.

"Yes, hullo?" said a polite male voice. It was funny how you could pick up an English accent even from such a small test sample.

I swallowed. "Hi, it's a friend of Gemma's from school? Mattie Monaghan?"

"I'm sorry, who?"

Erg. Of course she hadn't mentioned me. "Mattie—Matilda—Monaghan? I was at the Halloween party last night? At Willow Kaplan's house?"

Stop squeaking, I scolded myself.

"Oh, yes," said the voice. "Is Gemma expecting you?"

"No. Although maybe yes. She has something of mine. Well, technically it's my brother's—"

Gemma's father, or whoever it was, buzzed me in. I guess he wasn't interested in all the details.

The Braithwaites' apartment was on the third floor. I could have taken the elevator, but closed spaces make me claustrophobic, so I went up the stairs. By the time

I reached their door, I was breathless, and not just from nerves.

"Good morning," said a man who looked like Gemma (with stubble) and smelled like eggs. "Won't you come in?"

I took a step inside. "Thanks. I'm just here to pick up my little brother's—"

"Mattie! Good morning," said Gemma, walking toward the door. She was wearing a red plaid flannel robe, and her hair was wet, as if she'd just stepped out of the shower. If she was embarrassed to see me, it didn't show; she was smiling, but I detected question marks in her eyes.

"I came for the cape," I explained. "My little brother—"

"Oh, of course! The cape! So sorry! I should have rung you this morning!"

"No, it's fine. I wasn't answering my phone, anyway."

"Would you like a coffee? Or a cup of tea?" Gemma's dad asked.

"No thanks. Really, just the cape—"

"Gems, I believe your friend would like her *cape*," Gemma's dad said. He was smiling ironically. Was that British, or was he making fun of me?

"Right," Gemma said briskly. "Please come out to the balcony, Mattie. Don't mind the mess; Daddy and I are not much for housekeeping."

I followed her through their narrow living room, not much more than a beige tweed sofa littered with news-paper sections, a small blue rug, a bookshelf crammed with hardcovers, and a single brown leather chair. A dad's apartment: There were probably jars of pickles in the fridge, and maybe some bacon.

Gemma opened the door to the balcony, motioning me to step outside.

"I put the cape out here overnight so it would dry. I'm afraid there was a spill. What I mean is, *I* spilled orange soda. But I rinsed it out." She frowned as she sniffed the black fabric. "Still smells a bit orangey, but it's not sticky anymore, so that's progress, I suppose. I'm not the best at cleaning things."

"I'm sure it's fine."

"Anyway, sorry."

"For what?" I said. "*I* should be apologizing to *you*."

"For what?" She wrung her wet hair over one shoulder, looking at me with wide eyes and wet eyelashes.

I inhaled the chilly air. "I don't know. Not telling you who I was. In the kitchen."

"Mattie," Gemma said, smiling, "what's the point of wearing a costume if you go around explaining to every-one who you are?"

"Yes, but I didn't mean to *trick* anybody."

"You mean Willow? Well, serves her right for not inviting you!"

I caught my breath. So Gemma hadn't felt tricked—which meant she hadn't thought I was a boy. Hadn't been flirting with me, either. Well, that was a huge relief.

But why had I thought she was? I must have been delirious with nerves and thirst. Or light-headed from wearing that heavy, sweaty mask.

"Anyway," Gemma was saying, "I'm very sorry you had to sneak in. Can I ask you something? Why *didn't* Willow invite you?"

"I don't know. She hardly talks to us, except when there's a fight about something."

"Who's 'us'?"

"Lucy, Tessa, and me. Although for some reason she invited *them*."

"But not you? That's odd," Gemma said. "Did you offend her?"

"No. I don't think so. Truthfully, I'm not the offender type."

"I didn't think you were." She paused. "You know, Willow's not a bad person, really. She just likes being captain."

"You mean she likes excluding people."

"Oh, but that's not fair. She *couldn't* include everyone in her basement, could she? And I suppose she doesn't like surprises. You did surprise her, you know." Gemma laughed a little. "Anyhow, try not to mind her reaction. I'm sure it wasn't personal."

"How come everyone keeps saying that?" I said. "They'd think it was personal if it happened to *them*."

"I'm sure you're right about that," Gemma admitted.

"Gems!" Gemma's dad called from somewhere inside the apartment. "Time to ring your mum!"

"Bollocks," Gemma muttered. "It's the weekly phone call with Mummy. She's always furious if I'm five minutes late for it. You'd better go now." She handed me the cape. "Thanks again for letting me borrow it, Mattie. You saved my life."

"No problem," I said.

For a second I thought she might hug me again, the way some girls do. But she didn't. I turned and we walked back into the apartment, and then I was out the door and down the stairs, the cape feeling slightly sticky in my hands.

"For never was a story of more woe
Than this of Juliet and her Romeo."
—*Romeo and Juliet*, V.iii.310–311

I dreaded going to school on Monday, sure I was in for a day of teasing—plenty of *Star Wars* references, at the absolute least. Somehow I managed to convince Mom to drive me there as late as possible, just in time for the end of homeroom. As soon as I walked in, I could tell that everyone was buzzing—but not about me. About something else.

"What's going on?" I asked Tessa, who was practically bouncing in her seat.

"Eighth-grade play gets announced today," she answered.

"Really? How do you know?"

"Mr. Torres was just in here talking it up. You shouldn't have missed it. Why were you late? And guess what, Mattie? He's directing!"

He was? That was great news. Mr. Torres was our English teacher, and everyone agreed that he was the best. Lucy had Mrs. Dimona, who'd so far spent the entire semester on the first four chapters of *Animal Farm*, and gave weekly spelling tests, like they were second graders. The other class had Miss Bluestone, who was ancient and crazy, and talked about authors as if they were her former boyfriends. She never assigned any women writers except Emily Dickinson, who she referred to as just "Emily"—as if Emily Dickinson were some poetry-writing friend of hers who'd never been published.

But Mr. Torres was incredibly cool. And not just that: He got me. Whenever I raised my hand to ask a question, or to comment about some passage we were reading, Mr. Torres would smile at me in a special way that said: *Keep going. You're onto something. You're good at this, Mattie.* And I'd smile back—but behind my book, so no one could see it and accuse me of sucking up.

When the end-of-homeroom bell rang, I asked Tessa if Mr. Torres had mentioned which play.

She shook her head. "He said he'll tell us today in class. Tryouts are end of the week. But I can't wait that long; I'm so excited I think I may barf."

"Well, please don't, okay?"

She studied my face. "Speaking of barf . . . You're over the Halloween party thing?"

"I guess."

She groaned. "*I guess, I guess.* That's like your theme song lately."

"Well, sorry, Tessa. I just need time to think things out."

"No, you don't," Tessa said. "You only *think* you need to think. Just *act*, for once!"

"What are you talking about?" I scowled at her. "My costume disasters? Because you're right, I definitely over-thought those. I admit it, okay? But I act! I came to Willow's party, didn't I?"

She squeezed my arm. "Sheesh, Mattie. Chill, all right? I'm talking about Elijah. Stop analyzing how you feel about him and *decide.* Crush or no crush? Thumbs up or thumbs down?"

"Why do you care? And anyway, why *do* I need to choose?"

"Because everybody needs to choose *some*thing. To be *or* not to be; *that* is the question."

"I really don't think that's what Hamlet was talking about."

"Maybe not, but it's what *I'm* talking about." Tessa stepped into her math room. "See you in English," she said, kissing her fingers and waving bye-bye.

* * *

All day long, I thought about what Tessa had said—not about Elijah, but about the play. All the eighth graders had to participate, even if that meant painting scenery or running props. So what if I asked to be Mr. Torres's assistant? Maybe I could take notes while he rehearsed the actors, or help kids who'd messed up their lines.

Anyway, thinking about the play was a good distraction as I spent the day avoiding Willow and all her many teammates. I also avoided Elijah as much as I could—which wasn't easy, because he was in most of my classes. As for Gemma, it was funny how completely she'd vanished into her circle of friends. Not that I thought she'd leave a note in my locker (*Wanna sit together at lunch?*)—but on the balcony, it almost seemed as if she wanted to get to know me, or at least to understand why we *couldn't* be friends. Today, I'd seen her shiny brown braid a few times, and heard her laughing, but she was always at the center of a large group of kids. Team Willow, which I wasn't about to take on.

At lunch, Lucy and Tessa couldn't stop making predictions about the play. According to Tessa, the pattern went: musical, nonmusical, musical, non. Last year the eighth grade did *Grease*; the year before was *Our Town*; three years ago, *West Side Story*. So this year, it was time for a nonmusical, and wouldn't it be awesome if we did Shakespeare?

"Awesome for *you*," Lucy said. "Not for everyone else."

"How come?" Tessa demanded.

"Tessa, you're a Shakespeare geek. You do theater camp. You memorize insults—"

"Because they're hilarious! *Shakespeare's* hilarious! Can you think of a better choice?"

"Any musical," Lucy declared. "With choreography."

"That's because you're a dancer! So it's awesome for *you*!"

I let them argue while I ate an apple. But then Lucy asked what play I was rooting for. I answered that I didn't have one specifically in mind.

Tessa snorted. "There she goes again. *I guess. I can't decide. I'm staying neutral.*"

"Shut up," I told her, swatting her arm. "I don't know. Maybe a love story. Or something weird, like *The Bald Soprano*."

"The *who*? Mattie, *you're* weird."

I shrugged. The truth was, I knew that whatever play Mr. Torres chose would be perfect. He'd never waste our time on something boring or brainless. Also, I knew Tessa was picking on me only because she was nervous. But I still wished she'd stop.

Finally, it was time for English class. Mr. Torres took slow, casual steps into the classroom and grinned at us, as if he knew we were all waiting for his entrance, and he wanted to tease us a little first.

"Good afternoon, humans," he said. That's what he always called us: humans.

"Mr. Torres?" Tessa said. "We're going crazy. *Please* tell us what play we're doing, I beg you." She clasped her hands together and made her voice sound desperate. *Already she's auditioning*, I thought.

"Well, here's the thing," Mr. Torres said, leaning against his desk and folding his arms. "This year, I'm playing a dual role: teacher and director. But notice I put teacher first. So what I've done is pick a play I can teach and direct at the same time. We'll discuss it in class as great literature and rehearse it onstage as great drama. The other eighth-grade English classes will too, by the way."

From across the room, I could feel Tessa vibrating.

"Are you going to tell us the name of the play, or should we guess?" Keisha asked. "I'm guessing *Wicked*."

"Ooh, I love that play!" Charlotte squealed.

Mr. Torres smiled. "It's *Romeo and Juliet*, by William Shakespeare."

Tessa slapped her desk in victory.

Some kids, mostly boys, groaned.

"Aw, come on, Mr. Torres," Ajay said. "The eighth-grade play is supposed to be fun!"

"*Romeo and Juliet is* fun," Mr. Torres said. "Plenty of swordplay and jokes. And, of course, dare I say it, romance."

Ajay snorted.

"But it's really saaaad," Keisha wailed. "Because they both die at the end, right?"

"Right," Mr. Torres said. "It's a tragedy. Although it's also very funny."

"Yeah, if you like jokes from a thousand years ago," Liam said.

"More like four hundred, actually."

More groans.

"Humans, I have to say you're disappointing me," Mr. Torres said. "I thought you'd all be excited!"

"It's just really hard to get excited about a play we're not even going to understand," Willow said.

"Yeah," Charlotte said. "It's not even modern English."

"You know," Mr. Torres said, "I don't believe in telling students they're wrong—but seriously, folks, that's just wrong. First of all, Shakespeare pretty much *invented* modern English. Lots of words we use today—'eyeball,' 'gossip,' 'cold-blooded,' 'rant,' 'fashionable,' 'obscene,'— he used first. Second of all, *you'll* get this play better than your parents will. Better than your teachers will, including me. You know why? Because it's about *an eighth grader in love*."

Willow made a skeptical face. "It is?"

"Yep. Juliet is just thirteen years old, and her parents want to marry her off to some rich guy she doesn't even know."

"That's so weird," Liam said.

"But it wasn't weird for the times, right?" Tessa said.

Mr. Torres nodded. "But then she meets Romeo at a dance—actually, it's a costume party at her house, and Romeo sneaks in, disguised, and—thunderbolt!—they fall madly in love."

"How old is Romeo?" Elijah asked.

"Good question. Shakespeare doesn't say, but he's a teenager who hangs out with his friends and lives with his parents. Who, by the way, don't approve of Juliet's family. And vice versa."

"Is that why they die?" Keisha asked. She looked worried. "Because of their parents?"

"Well, that's basically the reason," Mr. Torres answered. "Romeo's family and Juliet's family hate each other, so, with the help of Friar Lawrence, the lovers come up with a secret plan to be together. Tragically, the plan backfires."

"How?" Keisha asked.

"Okay, let me back up a little. Romeo's friends Mercutio and Benvolio get into a sword fight with Juliet's cousin Tybalt, who's a hotheaded bully. Tybalt kills Mercutio when Romeo gets in the way trying to stop it. Then Romeo kills Tybalt in revenge, and as a punishment gets banished from Verona."

"What about Juliet?" Keisha pressed. "Does she go with him?"

"No, but Friar Lawrence marries them in secret just before Romeo leaves. And when Juliet's parents try to force her to marry the rich guy, Paris, she goes to Friar Lawrence, who gives her a poison that will make her *seem* dead for forty-two hours. His idea is, if Juliet is 'dead,' she doesn't have to marry Paris. Everybody with me?"

The class nodded.

"Okay." Mr. Torres sat on the edge of his desk. "So Friar Lawrence sends a note to Romeo explaining the plan, but unfortunately, there's a mix-up, and the note never arrives. So Romeo thinks Juliet really *is* dead and kills himself at her tomb. And when Juliet wakes up and sees Romeo is dead for real, she kills herself too."

"Fun times," Ajay grumbled.

"Well, as I said, there's plenty of humor. Mercutio is a lot of fun, and Juliet's Nurse—not a registered nurse, but a nursemaid, sort of like a nanny—is hilarious."

"Why do the families hate each other?" Willow asked.

Mr. Torres shrugged. "All we know is that they have an 'ancient grudge.' The reason isn't important. Why do people *ever* hate each other? It's usually not for anything rational or specific, right?"

"In *West Side Story* it's because they're different ethnic groups," Keisha said. "And the white kids think the Puerto Rican kids are taking their turf."

"Exactly. And you realize that *West Side Story* is an updated *Romeo and Juliet*, right?"

"But couldn't we just do *West Side Story* instead?" Charlotte pleaded.

"No, Charlotte, we could not," Mr. Torres replied. "And here's why: Because this is English class, and we're gonna English-class this play. Now let's get started, humans."

As Mr. Torres handed out paperback copies of *Romeo and Juliet*, I thought that Tessa might explode from excitement. Her face was pink, and she was bouncing in her seat while she turned the pages of the play, silently mouthing the words. Elijah was frowning as he read the first page; I remembered how he'd said he hated wearing costumes, and of course this was a costumey play. Willow, Charlotte, and Isabel were whispering to each other, probably deciding who would get which parts. Liam was sneaking a look at his phone, Ajay was staring out the window, and Keisha was peeking at the last few pages, her face pinched, as if she was afraid she might burst into tears.

And me? I caught Mr. Torres's eye. He smiled.

"Mattie, why don't you read aloud?" he said. "Act One, Scene One. Let's start with the chorus."

"I pray, sir, can you read?"
"Ay, mine own fortune in my misery."
—*Romeo and Juliet*, I.ii. 57–58

When school was over, Tessa declared she needed a cup of fro-yo or she'd die. I said maybe it was too soon to return to Verona's; Lucy said she thought enough time had passed, as long as we (she looked right at Tessa) kept our voices down and behaved. Finally, we agreed to go—but that if Willow or any of her friends showed up, we'd leave. No point risking another fight, and possibly even permanent banishment.

That day I got peanut butter with chocolate chips, Lucy got mango with chopped strawberries, and Tessa got a combination of Oreo and banana with mini-marshmallows, Raisinets, gumdrops, and crushed pretzels. (I know.)

I watched her shove a giant spoonful into her mouth. "O, Oreo, Oreo, wherefore art thou Oreo?" she said. "That which we call a fro-yo by any other name would taste as sweet— Hey, guys, don't you think I'd be a perfect Juliet?"

"Is that the part you want?" I asked, avoiding her question.

"Obviously," Tessa said. "Who doesn't?"

She had a point. At dismissal I'd heard a bunch of girls from Mrs. Dimona's class talking about auditions. Competition for Juliet was going to be insane.

I glanced at Lucy, who was making winding roads in her strawberries with the tip of her spoon. "What about you?"

"I don't know," she said, blushing.

"That means Juliet, right?" Tessa asked. "Come on, Lucy Goosey, admit it."

Lucy shrugged. "I was thinking about it, I guess. But I'll never get it. I really hope you do, Tessa. Although everyone in my class was talking about that English girl."

"You mean Gemma?" I asked, a little too quickly.

Lucy looked at me. "Yeah. They said she's been in a bunch of Shakespeare productions at her old school. Plus, she has that accent."

"So what?" Tessa scoffed. "We're doing an American version, right?"

"Okay, but it's more than just the accent. Don't you think Gemma Braithwaite *looks* like a Juliet?"

I swallowed some fro-yo. "What does that mean?"

"You know," Lucy said. "She's really, really pretty."

"Anyone can be pretty onstage," Tessa argued. "That's what costumes and makeup are for! And I bet Lady Gemma's a wad of snot."

"Don't say that," I said. "She happens to be incredibly nice."

Tessa raised her eyebrows. "Yeah? Based on what?"

"I talked to her at the party."

"Gemma was at Willow's party?" Lucy frowned. "I didn't see her there."

"Right, because she was hiding in the kitchen. She didn't have a costume, so . . ." I shoved some fro-yo into my mouth.

"Wait," Tessa said, waving her spoon like a baton. "Stop, Mattie. How do you know she was in the kitchen? Were *you* in the kitchen?"

"Yeah."

"So you penetrated the Kaplans' inner sanctum? And that's where Willow exposed your identity?"

I nodded.

"Ha! She must have gone ballistic on you. Well, that explains the barf."

"Shut up, Tessa." Lucy sighed. "Anyhow, I'm glad to hear Gemma is nice."

"*I'm* not," Tessa said. "Because if she's talented and experienced *and* nice *and* pretty, she's definitely Juliet."

"Tessa, you're all of that stuff, anyway," I told her. "And besides, who says Juliet has to be pretty?"

Tessa licked some fro-yo off her spoon. "Hey, Mattie, come on, you heard Mr. Torres. He called it a lightning bolt, the way Romeo falls in love with her at the party. It wouldn't make sense if Juliet's ugly."

"Why not?" I argued. "People fall in love for lots of reasons."

"You mean like because of someone's *eyebrows*?" Tessa snorted. "No offense, Mattie, but you really don't know the first thing about romance, do you?"

Way back in the fourth grade, our class put on a play called *A Voyage to Ellis Island*. Most of the other kids played immigrants with names like Giuseppe and Malka and Sean, or else they were Ellis Island workers in plain gray uniforms. There were no tryouts; our teacher, Mrs. Gustafson, just assigned us parts.

The part she gave me was the Narrator. I had a lot of lines to say, but no costume. I could just wear my normal clothes onstage, Mrs. Gustafson said.

"But the Narrator is boring," I told her. "Can't I have a real character?" By that I meant one with a foreign name, a head scarf, and a long skirt. I wasn't a costumey sort of person, even then, but if someone *made* me a costume, I'd gladly wear it.

Mrs. Gustafson took me aside and spoke quietly. "Oh, but Mattie, the Narrator has many important facts to share with the audience. We need someone who'll say them all correctly."

She meant it as a compliment, I guess. But the way I took it was: *You're a good reader, Mattie, and a smart girl. But you aren't the actor type.*

All through middle school, I never auditioned for anything. Because what was the point? If you're in a play, you want to be *in* the play, not standing outside it, in your normal clothes, narrating. And if I wasn't the actor type, okay. There were worse things to call a person. I wasn't even jealous of Tessa's theater camp, or of Lucy's dancing.

But that afternoon, when I got home from Verona's and locked myself in my bedroom to read *Romeo and Juliet*, something happened to me. It was kind of a thunderbolt, I guess you could call it. Because as I was reading, I started speaking the words out loud, feeling the characters' emotions as if they were mine. I didn't understand every word, and a few times I skimmed when certain characters (specifically, Mercutio and Friar Lawrence) got speechy. But the idea that Romeo and Juliet had a secret love they had

to hide from their families, even from their best friends—
it was a story so real I could almost see it happening in
front of me.

And when I got to the end, when Juliet discovers that
Romeo is dead, and kisses his lips, and they're still warm,
I did the whole scene in front of the mirror, including the
kiss. My eyes had actual tears, and I thought: *It's like this
play is happening TO me. Inside me.*

I wanted to own it. I wanted to *eat* it, as if it were chocolate layer cake.

So I started memorizing little chunks of it, like when
Romeo tells Friar Lawrence that being banished would
feel like torture:

> Heaven is here,
> Where Juliet lives, and every cat and dog
> And little mouse, every unworthy thing,
> Live here in heaven and may look on her;
> But Romeo may not. (III.iii.29–33)

And when Juliet says:

> Give me my Romeo; and when he shall die,
> Take him and cut him out in little stars,
> And he will make the face of heaven so fine

That all the world will be in love with night
And pay no worship to the garish sun.
(III.ii.21–25)

I said these speeches in front of my mirror, over and over. And then I wondered: If I *got* this play and *felt* these things and passionately *loved* these gorgeous words, didn't that mean I should try out for a part?

No, I told myself. *I'm a reader, not an actor; acting and reading are completely different things!*

But I couldn't make myself believe it. By then I knew, really knew in my stomach, that I needed to be onstage, in costume, not off to the side, excluded. Not "assisting" Mr. Torres or painting scenery. Not narrating. And not just reading, either. I had to be *in* this play. A part of it.

And the fact that Gemma Braithwaite might possibly get the role of Juliet?

Maybe we'd even get to be friends, or something.

10

"But to himself so secret and so close."
—*Romeo and Juliet*, I.i.152

For the rest of that week, Mr. Torres had our class read the play aloud. By the way he was paying attention, I could tell he was starting to think about casting, even before Friday's tryouts. So every time he chose me to read, I put a lot of extra emotion into my voice. I hadn't decided which part I wanted, but I was pretty sure which parts I didn't. I even made a list in my English notebook:

Romeo: Too important.

Juliet: Ditto. Too much competition.

Tybalt (Juliet's cousin): Too much action, too
  much shouting.

Mercutio: Funny, but too speechy
  (the whole Queen Mab thing).

Juliet's Nurse : Really funny, but all the
        girls who don't get Juliet will want!
        Second-best girl part.
Lord Capulet: Too mean.
Lady Capulet: Too wimpy/mean.
        Third-biggest girl part, so competition.
Friar Lawrence: Too speechy. Responsible
        for the sad ending. ☹
Prince: Boring.
Chorus: Narrator in tights! ☹

Mr. Torres had told us that the fact that there were only
four female roles—Juliet, Lady Capulet, the Nurse, and Lady
Montague—wasn't important. Everyone was eligible for
every role, male or female—but eliminating all these characters didn't leave me much. I could be one of Romeo's parents
(Lord Montague had more lines than Lady Montague, but
they were both pretty blah), or somebody's servant, or Paris
(the rich guy Juliet's parents want her to marry instead of
Romeo), or Benvolio, Romeo's cousin and best friend. Of all
of these, Benvolio was definitely the best part, but a couple of
times I heard Lucy say that *she* was hoping for Benvolio, and
obviously, I didn't want to compete against Lucy. I also could
have been a Party Guest or a Townsperson, which would
have allowed me to wear a girl's costume, at least—but they

had no lines, and I definitely wanted a speaking role. Saying Shakespeare's actual *words* was the entire point.

But which words? By Thursday night I needed to make a decision, because for tryouts we were supposed to prepare a speech. Mr. Torres warned that just because we recited a certain character's lines didn't mean we'd be considered to play that character—but he said he'd "take note of our choice of role," whatever that meant.

"Elijah wants to play Juliet's Nurse," Ajay announced in class on Wednesday.

Elijah blushed. "Only if you're Juliet, moron."

"Mr. Torres," Willow said. "It's really not fair that girls have to play boys. There should be more girl parts."

"Take it up with Shakespeare," Mr. Torres said. "But, you know, in Shakespeare's day, the female parts were played by boys. It might have been hard for him to cast those parts, which could explain why he wrote relatively few. Anyway, I encourage *all* of you to consider *all* roles—although I have to say, I'd like to cast a boy from this class as Romeo."

LIAM, Tessa mouthed at me from across the room.

I shrugged at her. Liam Harrison looked like someone's *idea* of a Romeo, with his yellow-blond hair and his square cleft chin; but whenever he read aloud, *splat*. It was like all the air went whooshing out of Shakespeare's lines. Really, considering Tessa's own overdramatic ways, I didn't get how she couldn't hear it.

But Tessa wasn't the only one casting the play before tryouts. All week long, I kept hearing how Keisha would be an awesome Nurse, and wouldn't Elijah make the perfect Friar Lawrence? I ignored this kind of talk for the most part—until on Thursday afternoon, in the PE locker room, I heard Lexi Barker telling Nicole Rizzi how "Willow would totally rock Juliet."

I froze. Had Willow *said* she wanted to play Juliet? I knew if she had, none of her crew would compete against her—and, of course, her crew included Gemma Braithwaite. The thought that Gemma might not get to play Juliet, might not even show up tomorrow to try out for a part that was so obviously meant for *her*, gave me a strange prickly feeling in my chest.

I had to find out. But I had no way to talk to Gemma in private. I certainly wasn't going to call her landline, or show up at her house and ring the buzzer.

Finally, at dismissal on Thursday, I asked Lucy if Tessa still wanted to play Juliet.

"Yeah, I think so," Lucy said. "Why?"

"What about Gemma?" I asked.

"What about Gemma *what*?" Lucy cocked her head as if she had water in her ear or something.

I looked away. "I mean, I thought you said people were talking about Gemma playing Juliet. Remember? And Tessa said she'd never get it, because Gemma was so pretty. And talented, and everything. So is Gemma not trying out? Because if Tessa *is*—"

"I don't know, Mattie." Lucy sounded as if she hadn't been following my logic. Maybe she hadn't even been listening. "So are you coming to tryouts?"

"Me?" I stared at her. I hadn't said anything about wanting a part; how had Lucy figured it out?

She smiled. "I mean to cheer us on. I've never been this nervous about anything in my life!"

Of course, that was when I should have told her I'd be there—but to try out for a part. For myself. Except I hadn't even picked my audition speech yet, so I wasn't ready to answer questions. Also, I knew she'd immediately tell Tessa, and then I'd have to deal with Tessa's pinball energy, and maybe hear how acting was all about *feelings* and *action*, and was I sure I was really the actor type, especially since I didn't know a thing about romance? And instead of spending the afternoon picking a speech, and then practicing it all evening, I'd be spending all that time texting back and forth with Tessa, and probably also getting a long, nervous phone call from Lucy.

"Did you hear what I said?" Lucy poked me. "Or are you spacing?"

"Sorry," I told her. "Yes, I'll definitely be there."

"Yay! Thanks!"

She gave me a best-friend hug, and I hugged her back.

Finally, it was time for tryouts. When school was over on Friday, all eighth graders who wanted to audition were supposed to show up in the auditorium with a copy of the play. Lucy and Tessa had told me to meet them by the doors, and we'd all go in together.

Obviously, this was my absolute last chance to tell them I planned to audition. So I did.

I told Tessa first, because she was the first to arrive.

She just blinked at me. "Oh," she finally said. "Well, Mattie, that's a surprise."

"Why is it a surprise?"

"*Why?* First of all, because you never audition for anything. Ever."

Then Lucy ran over. "What's going on?" she asked immediately. Tessa told her.

"You *are?*" Lucy asked me. She traded looks with Tessa.

"What's the big deal?" I managed a small, hollow laugh. "I thought you guys would be happy for me!"

"We are," Lucy said. "It's just weird how you never said anything."

I shrugged. "You didn't ask."

"Oh, we have to *ask*?" Tessa said. "We can't just have a conversation about which parts we want and expect that you'll, you know, *join in*? Be honest with us? Share *information*?"

Her voice was too loud; people were staring at us as they walked into the auditorium.

"Well, I'm sorry," I said. "When we were having fro-yo on Monday, I hadn't read the play yet. I only decided to try out once I'd read it that afternoon."

"You could have told us then," Lucy said softly. "Or the whole rest of this week. Or yesterday, when we were talking about it, Mattie."

Mrs. Dimona walked by, carrying a stack of pages. "Girls, please sit. We're starting in five minutes."

"We'd better go," Lucy said, not moving.

I looked at my friends, who were both frowning. Lucy was twisting her hair, watching me with hurt eyes. All of a sudden, I understood what they were both feeling, and I felt ashamed of myself.

"Listen, guys," I started. "I'm sorry, okay? I didn't mean to keep it a secret from you. I just needed a little time to—"

"Think?" Tessa finished.

"Decide. On which speech."

"And inform us afterward. Like you did with that Darth Vader costume."

"What? Tessa, that was a completely different . . ."

But then Willow and her entourage showed up, so I stopped talking, and the three of us took our seats inside the auditorium.

11

"O, he's a lovely gentleman!
Romeo's a dishclout to him."
—*Romeo and Juliet*, III.v.220–221

Two hours later, tryouts were over.

Most of it went by in a blur. About thirty girls showed up to recite "O Romeo, Romeo, wherefore art thou Romeo?"—which starts to sound like Bugs Bunny if you hear it too often. Tessa did Juliet's reaction when the Nurse tells her that Romeo killed Tybalt ("O serpent heart, hid with a flow'ring face!") probably because it sounded like insults. Lucy read a speech by Benvolio, Elijah read Friar Lawrence, Ajay read Lord Capulet, and Willow read Tybalt. They all did fine, I thought, and Keisha was hilarious as the Nurse.

But the truth was, I focused mainly on Gemma Braithwaite, who walked onstage slowly, taking her time. She was wearing a dark blue sweater and a dark red skirt.

Her braid had a pink streak in it—was it a ribbon? Her hair? I squinted, but I couldn't tell.

She cleared her throat, paused, and peered out at the audience. Was she searching for someone? I looked around, wondering who it was.

"Gemma's so Juliet," I heard Charlotte say behind me. "She shouldn't even have to try out."

"I know, right?" Isabel replied. "WOO! GO, GEMMA!"

I turned around and glared. "Will you please be quiet? She's trying to concentrate."

"Well, sor-ree," Charlotte said.

Lucy glanced at me. I pretended not to notice.

Gemma took a breath and spoke:

"Give me my Romeo; and when he shall die,
Take him and cut him out in little stars,
And he will make the face of heaven so fine
That all the world will be in love with night
And pay no worship to the garish sun."

I couldn't believe it. My favorite lines from the play, words I'd memorized, and Gemma had chosen them! It was almost as if we'd had a conversation about it beforehand— or, no, as if we hadn't needed one. As if we could read each other's minds. Was that even possible?

And her voice. It was perfect for Juliet—a little whispery, but strong at the same time. She didn't even lose her breath once, maybe because she'd had experience acting. And when she said "cut him out in little stars" you could hear all the *t* sounds, one by one, like a pair of scissors snipping.

It was as if Shakespeare had written the part just for her.

"Whoa," Tessa murmured when Gemma finished.

I watched Gemma take her seat next to Willow, who gave her a high five as if she'd just blocked a ball from scoring. From behind me, Isabel shouted, "WOOHOO, GEMMA, ALL RIGHT," and Charlotte jabbed my shoulder.

"Okay with you if we talk?" she asked. "Gemma's done now."

I shrugged her off. Again, Lucy turned to look at me. Again, I kept my eyes staring straight ahead, pretending to listen as Liam recited a Romeo speech, with hand gestures. When he finished, he bowed to applause from some girls in the front row. Mrs. Dimona and Miss Bluestone, who were sitting onstage behind Mr. Torres, were both beaming. I didn't even want to know Tessa's reaction.

Then Mr. Torres called out my name. I was next.

I stood. My heart was banging. I felt cold, and a little dizzy.

"You'll do great," Lucy said. Tessa gave my back a sharp pat as I walked past.

I climbed three steps to the stage. Mr. Torres was sitting on a stool, scribbling in a notebook.

He looked up when I was center stage. "So what have you prepared for us today?" he asked, his voice sounding cheery but also tired.

"Um, Paris," I said softly.

"Excuse me?"

"Paris," I answered, louder this time. "It's what he says to Romeo in Act Five, when Romeo comes to Juliet's tomb, and Paris thinks Juliet died out of grief for her cousin Tybalt, who Romeo killed to get back at Tybalt for killing Mercutio. Also, he thinks Romeo is at Juliet's tomb to vandalize it, so he wants to kill Romeo. Who shouldn't even be there, because he's been banished for killing Tybalt."

Mr. Torres smiled. "Yes, that's right, Mattie. How do you know all that?"

"I read the play."

"The whole thing? On your own?"

I nodded.

"Nice," Mr. Torres said. "But where's your book?"

"I don't need it. I memorized the speech. Paris is my favorite character, and I'd really, really like to play him."

"Would you?" He scribbled something. "Well, go ahead, then, please."

I looked out into the auditorium. but I couldn't see Lucy or Tessa, not even Gemma's pink braid. Although maybe that was a good thing.

I took a deep breath and said:

> "This is that banish'd haughty Montague
> That murdered my love's cousin—with which grief
> It is supposed the fair creature died—
> And here is come to do some villainous shame
> To the dead bodies. I will apprehend him.
> Stop thy unhallow'd toil, vile Montague!
> Can vengeance be pursu'd further than death?
> Condemned villain, I do apprehend thee.
> Obey, and go with me; for thou must die."

When I finished, I cringed a little, because to me the last two lines came out sounding Darth Vader–ish, like I was waving a lightsaber and saying them into the voice thingy. I peeked at Mr. Torres, who was writing again in his notebook.

I waited, my insides squirming. Finally, he looked up at me. "Mattie? Can you hang around afterward for a bit?"

I swallowed. "Sure."

Then I sat down again. Lucy patted my knee. "You did great," she murmured. And Tessa leaned across Lucy and whispered, "That was awesome. He wants you to stay after? What for?"

"He didn't say."

Charlotte poked me from behind. "Teacher's pet," she teased in a singsong voice that was meant to sound babyish, like she was making fun of a kid calling me that. But still, she was calling me that.

And, of course, Tessa heard. "Shut up, you *pukestocking*," she hissed at Charlotte.

"Excuse me?" Charlotte said. "What did you just call me?"

"It's Shakespeare, but even *you* can figure it out. So watch what you call my friend, you *mildewed ear*." Tessa nodded at me. "*Hamlet*," she said, knowing I'd ask where the quote was from.

A few more kids auditioned. When they finished, and tryouts were officially over, Lucy asked if I wanted her to wait. I said no; whatever Mr. Torres wanted to talk to me about sounded private. So Tessa, Lucy, and I hugged each other.

"Sorry for not saying anything about the tryout," I told them.

My friends waved me away, acting like they'd completely forgotten our fight by now. Then they both took off.

I waited in my seat for Mr. Torres to finish chatting with Mrs. Dimona and Miss Bluestone. The whole time, my stomach was twisting, dreading what he'd say: *Mattie, you're a great reader, and a smart girl, but you aren't the actor type. How would you like to be the Chorus? Or, better yet, why don't you paint the scenery?*

Finally, the other teachers left, and he jumped off the stage, taking a seat two rows in front of me. "So, here's a question for you, Mattie," he said. "Why do you want to play Paris?"

"I'm not sure," I replied. "I just think he's kind of cool."

Mr. Torres scratched his chin. "You know, I've been reading, teaching, and directing this play for the past fifteen years, and no student of mine has *ever* thought Paris was *cool*. Why not aim higher?"

"What do you mean?"

"I mean, I'd like you to consider a bigger part. How about Friar Lawrence, for example? Or Lord Capulet? Or maybe Benvolio?"

But Benvolio is Lucy's. "No thanks."

"How come? You'd be great, Mattie. You read with so much understanding, and memorizing is clearly not an issue."

"I just don't want such a big part. I *like* Paris. I feel sorry for him. I think he loves Juliet, even though she's not interested."

Mr. Torres smiled. "Well, you'll make a terrific Paris.

Don't tell anyone I said that. The cast list's not official until Monday."

"Okay," I said, beaming. "I promise."

He stood. Just as he took a step toward the stage, I blurted: "Mr. Torres? I really think Gemma Braithwaite should play Juliet."

He stopped. "Do you?"

"Definitely. She's the best. She's done Shakespeare before, so she has experience, and I really just think . . ." I could hear myself repeating. *Breathe, Mattie.* "I mean, I want this play to be good."

"That makes two of us, then." He winked at me. "Thanks for the input. Anything else?"

"No. Actually, wait: Did you think I sounded like Darth Vader? Especially when I said the last two lines?"

Mr. Torres laughed. "Maybe a bit. But I'm pretty sure the force is with you, so I wouldn't sweat it too much, Mattie."

"Parting is such sweet sorrow."
—*Romeo and Juliet*, II.ii.185

I didn't see my friends that weekend, because my big sister, Cara, came to visit. She didn't come home very often, because she went to college three states away—and also, whenever she did show up, she always got into a major argument with Mom. Sometimes Cara brought a few of her college friends home with her, but the extra guests didn't stop Cara and Mom from arguing—about Cara's classes, grades, clothing, spending allowance, and Mom's cooking, work schedule, failure to recycle.

These fights were always loud, full of slammed doors and shouting, but they were even worse back when Cara was in middle school. At least, that's the way I remember them from when I was a preschooler. I remember once back then they were both shouting so much (after Cara got caught skipping PE class) that I went up to the attic so I wouldn't have to listen. And as soon as Mom realized she couldn't find me, she got frantic, yelling my name so loudly as she raced around the house that I thought she was mad at *me*. She must have heard me rustling something overhead, or walking, because eventually there she was in the attic, bursting into tears and hugging me so tight it was hard to breathe.

The funny thing was that afterward Cara was furious at me. "Why'd you have to scare Mom like that?" she scolded me. "Don't *ever* do that to her again!"

But you hate her, I thought. *Don't you?*

Anyway, the college visits always ended with Cara taking me out to breakfast at Patsy's Diner. We would order French toast, Cara would tell me about some professor she thought was a genius (or a monster), gossip about her roommate, and complain about Mom's "ridiculous standards." Then she'd drive me over to school, where I'd be late.

Don't tell Mom, she'd always say.

Don't worry, I won't, I'd always promise.

We'd rub noses. Then Cara would drive off, and I wouldn't see her again for three or four months—sometimes longer if she stayed with her father in California, a guy Mom had married for three years after college and divorced before she met Dad.

This time Cara arrived on her own, without friends to hide behind. For the first half hour of her visit, everything was fine. Then Mom asked a question about a jacket Cara had bought with a credit card, and Cara accused Mom of not trusting her. From there, it all went downhill, and none of the rest of us—Dad, Kayden, Mason, and me—could keep them from sniping at each other.

But on that Monday morning in the diner, as Cara and I finished our French toast, she looked at me with calm, wide eyes. I couldn't help thinking that once she was outside our house, Cara's face relaxed, and she almost looked like a different person.

"So what's up with you these days, little sister?" she asked, as if she really wanted to know.

"With me?" I said.

"Yeah. You seem a little . . . distracted."

"Sorry."

"Don't apologize. I'm just wondering about you. Everything okay?"

I swirled my French toast in a puddle of syrup. "Everything's fine. We're doing *Romeo and Juliet* as the eighth-grade play this year, and today we're getting the cast list, so . . ."

"Ah. You're nervous?"

"Not really. I already know my part."

"Don't tell me, let me guess. You're Juliet."

I laughed. "Don't be crazy, Cara."

"Why is that crazy? You'd make an awesome Juliet. And then that boy you like could be Romeo, and you'd have to kiss—"

"You mean Elijah?"

"Yeah, if that's his name. That boy you told me about last time—"

"Right. Elijah." I sipped some OJ. "The thing is, I'm not sure I still like him."

"Really? What happened?"

"Nothing *happened*. I just . . ." I looked away.

She reached across the table and stole a piece of my French toast. "You just what?"

"I don't know. How do you know if you like someone because you really do like that person, or if you like him only because you think you're supposed to?"

"Huh," Cara said, sitting back in her seat. "That's a tough one. With me, I usually like someone if I think I'm *not* supposed to like him. Like, see that guy with the cream cheese mustache?"

She rolled her eyes in the direction of a fat, bald, old man eating a bagel in the grossest, messiest way possible.

"If you told me, *Cara, you are under no circumstances supposed to have a crush on that disgusting guy over there; I absolutely forbid it*, I would find a way to fall passionately in love with him." She shuddered. "But why would you think you're *supposed* to like somebody?"

"I don't know. It's stupid. And maybe I still do like him, anyway. I don't know."

"Not that I'm counting, but you said *I don't know* three times."

"I did?"

"Yep. I just think if you really *do* like a person, it's not something you worry about. Or wonder about. You just *like* that person." She finished her coffee and checked her phone. "Shoot, it's late. I need to get you over to school."

We left the diner. She dropped me off at school, rolled down the window of her car so we could rub noses, and then she drove away.

By the time I arrived at school, homeroom was over, so I had to go to the main office to sign in late. I was supposed to go straight to first-period math, which had started eight minutes earlier, and which was *not* my best subject. My teacher, Mr. Peltz, was the nightmarish combination of hard and boring; as much as I tried to keep awake in his class, I kept spacing out. Which meant I'd barely passed the first two tests of the year, something my parents weren't letting me forget.

Even so, I decided to take a detour to the auditorium, just in case Mr. Torres had posted the cast list. Sure enough, there it was, taped to the auditorium doors.

Cast List for <u>Romeo and Juliet</u>

Chorus	Samantha Calabrese
Escalus, Prince of Verona	Bennett Park
Paris, a young nobleman	Matilda Monaghan
Montague, head of one house, at odds with Capulets	Drea Crawford
Capulet, head of one house, at odds with Montagues	Ajay Vehta
An old man, of the Capulet family	Emily Packer
Romeo, son to Montague	Liam Harrison
Tybalt, nephew to Lady Capulet	Willow Kaplan
Mercutio, kinsman to the Prince and friend to Romeo	Tessa Pollack
Benvolio, nephew to Montague and friend to Romeo	Lucy Yang
Friar Lawrence, a Franciscan	Elijah Simmons
Friar John, a Franciscan	Jake Martinez
Balthasar, servant to Romeo	Callie Brenner

Abram, servant to Montague	Ellie Yamaguchi
Sampson, servant to Capulet	Lexi Barker
Gregory, servant to Capulet	Nicole Rizzi
Peter, servant to Juliet's Nurse	Molly Cho
Lady Montague, wife to Montague	Isabel Guzman
Lady Capulet, wife to Capulet	Charlotte Pangel
Juliet, daughter to Capulet	Gemma Braithwaite
Nurse to Juliet	Keisha Bromley

I took a few minutes to let the list sink in.

I'm Paris; Gemma is Juliet. YES! I felt like shouting, or punching the air in victory.

Also, Lucy was Romeo's trusty cousin Benvolio—and Tessa was Mercutio, which was perfect, considering the hammy way they both acted. And I could totally imagine Ajay as nasty Lord Capulet, Willow as bossy Tybalt, and smiley Keisha as the Nurse. I even had to admit that Elijah would make a decent Friar Lawrence; anyway, there was no one better for that part.

But Liam Harrison as Romeo? Seriously? He just wasn't *dramatic* enough. There was no other way to think about it. When he read Romeo's lines in class, it was like his mind switched channels in the middle. And by the time he got to the end of a speech, he didn't even care about what he was saying.

And the thought that Gemma would be acting opposite him—Gemma, who at tryouts said Juliet's words as if she personally meant every syllable, every *t* sound—it was sickening, really.

How could Mr. Torres have messed up so badly?

13

"Give leave awhile, we must talk in secret."
—*Romeo and Juliet*, I.iii. 7–8

All day long, people were celebrating, or acting like good sports, or consoling each other, or pretending they didn't care about being cast as a citizen or a costume ball dancer. Tessa did a pseudo-pout about not getting Juliet, and having to play, as she put it, "a dude," but I knew her too well not to see that she was thrilled at getting Mercutio, a fun, funny character who even got to die in a jokey way. And Lucy, who was the least show-offy person on the planet, spent the rest of that Monday beaming, accepting congratulations from kids and teachers as if she'd never doubted she'd get Benvolio.

I didn't see Gemma, but I heard zero complaints that she'd been chosen for Juliet; after tryouts on Friday, I guess people just assumed she'd get the part. As for Liam, he acted almost embarrassed about being Romeo. For the rest of that day, boys were making kissy faces at him, and he kept scowling and saying rude things back. But I didn't feel sorry for him. I refused to.

When the whole cast met in the auditorium after dismissal, Mr. Torres told us he had a prediction: "When you are all ancient citizens contemplating your sadly misspent youths, participating in this production is the only thing you'll remember about middle school. The *only* thing. Nothing else: not your soccer practices or your math quizzes or who you sat with at lunch."

"I'll remember Tessa's body odor," Ajay said.

"I'll remember your mouth, you carcass fit for hounds," Tessa said. "*Julius Caesar*," she added, like it was a hashtag.

Everyone laughed. Tessa stood up and bowed. *Getting to play Mercutio is great for her, but maybe she should watch it with all the Shakespeare insults,* I thought.

And where was Gemma? Mr. Torres had already started handing out rehearsal schedules, but she wasn't sitting anywhere in the auditorium.

"Okay," Mr. Torres was saying. "Here's how it works. We open the weekend before Valentine's Day. So, not counting all the upcoming vacations and holidays, we have about twelve weeks of actual rehearsal—fourteen weeks all together—which is a lot less time than it sounds. Look for the name of your character on the calendar. Unless I let you know otherwise, you need to attend rehearsal only on the days your character has a scene. Of course, you're encouraged to attend any rehearsal. We're always grateful for an audience. . . . Ah. Let's all give a warm welcome to the star of our show, Miss Gemma Braithwaite." He gestured like a TV emcee.

Gemma came jogging down the aisle. "Sorry I'm late, Mr. Torres."

"No worries. But let's not make a habit of it, please."

"Oh, I won't. Really *very* sorry." She flopped into the seat next to me, panting slightly. Something flowery wafted off her body, a sweet-smelling wave of air. I inhaled. Was it perfume? No, my mom smelled like perfume. This was something else.

"Do you think he's angry at me?" she whispered.

"Mr. Torres?" I asked stupidly. "No. But he doesn't like lateness."

"Too bad for me, then, because I'm *always* late."

"You could set your phone to remind you."

"I could. But then I'd have to remember to set my phone."

Lucy, two seats away, glanced over at us with raised eyebrows. I pretended not to notice.

"What's this calendar about?" Gemma was asking.

"Rehearsals," I whispered. "He just gave it out."

"And I missed it? Bollocks. Can I look on with you?" She leaned over to read my calendar as Mr. Torres talked about the schedule. The funny thing was that her closeness and her scent made my head all swimmy. Like maybe I was allergic to her shampoo.

"Blimey," Gemma was murmuring. "I have to come to every rehearsal, don't I?"

"Well, not *every* one," I said. "And you're the lead, so . . ."

"I suppose. You're Paris, aren't you?" She scanned the schedule with her pointer finger. "Ooh, look, Mattie, we have a scene together."

"Act Four, Scene One," I said immediately. Then I blushed.

Gemma looked at me and smiled. "Ace memory."

"Not really. I'm only in five scenes, so it's really easy to—"

"Girls?" From the stage, Mr. Torres was looking at us questioningly. "Are you confused about something?"

"Not at all." Gemma smiled at him. "We're with you, Mr. Torres."

We're, I thought. She'd used the first-person plural.

Then Mr. Torres announced that he believed in "diving right in." So after laying out some ground rules for the next twelve weeks (including No Lateness), he asked the kids who were in Act One, Scene One to come up onstage.

"The rest of you can stay," he said. "In fact, you're *welcome* to stay, as I said. But if I were you, I'd go home and get some homework done. When the calendar says it's your scene, I expect your full attention here. Don't tell me, *Oh, Mr. Torres, I have a French test tomorrow*, or *Sorry, Mr. Torres, but I need to work on my English essay*. For the next fourteen weeks, aside from schoolwork, humans, play practice is your top priority."

Gemma leaned into me again. "Is he always such an ogre?" she murmured.

I was about to protest that Mr. Torres wasn't an ogre at all, he just wanted the show to be good, despite the fact that he'd chosen Liam Harrison for Romeo. But immediately Gemma was surrounded by her friends, who transported her out of the auditorium as if they were pirates and she were stolen treasure.

14

"*I will make thee think thy swan a crow.*"
—*Romeo and Juliet*, I.ii.89

Benvolio was in Act One, Scene One, so Lucy stayed to rehearse that first day, and Tessa and I walked home together. She was even more hyper than usual, going on and on about how cool it was to play Mercutio, how he had all the best lines in the play. I let her talk, my brain still swimming from the whispered conversation with Gemma. Not that we'd discussed anything personal or profound. But the way she knew I was playing Paris, the way she leaned over my calendar, as if she knew I wouldn't mind sharing, the way she'd said *we're*—it gave me hope that we could actually be friends. Despite the swarm of pirates who'd spirited her away.

"Well?" Tessa was staring at me.

"Well, what?"

"Mattie, you're being spacey again," Tessa complained. "Didn't you hear my question?"

"Sorry. Guess not."

She rolled her eyes. "I was just asking what you and Gemma were talking about."

"Oh. Actually, we were discussing the rehearsal calendar."

"Really? You two seemed chummier than *that*."

I could feel my cheeks heat up. "We aren't 'chummy.' And I only met her at Willow's house last week."

"Just be careful," Tessa said. "Willow can be crazy possessive. I think she's mad at *me* because I danced with Liam at her party. Like every girl in the *grade* wasn't dancing with him, you know?"

I thought it would be smart to change the subject. "You know, Willow kills you in the play," I pointed out. "Tybalt kills Mercutio in a sword fight. And then Romeo kills Tybalt for revenge, which is how he gets banished."

"Poor Romeo; he's such a screwup," Tessa said absentmindedly. She went quiet for a full block. Then she blurted: "So does she like him?"

"Does who like who? Does Juliet like Romeo?"

"No, you purple-hued malt-worm. I mean, does Gemma like Liam?"

"How would I know?"

"You talk to her. She talks to you."

"Hardly ever. And not about *Liam*."

"Mattie, come on. I need to know. And who else would I ask? Willow?" She shuddered.

"So you're saying I should ask Gemma? But I barely know her, Tessa."

"You know her better than I do! And all my scenes are with Lucy and Liam; I won't even see her at rehearsals. Obi-Wan Kenobi, you're my only hope. Pleeeease?" She did that pleading thing with her hands.

I pretended not to notice. "Tessa, why do you even care who she likes?"

"Why? I'll tell you why. Because she's going to have to kiss Liam, right? *A lot.* And since we all agree Gemma is pretty and nice and talented and English, it would help if she kind of hated Liam's guts."

"Fine." I said it just to shut her up. "I'll see what I can find out. But I'm not promising anything. And don't bug me about it, okay?"

"I'll be quiet as a mouse. Hey, I wonder if that's a Will."

I looked at her. "A what?"

"An expression Shakespeare invented. Like *mind's eye* or *all's well that ends well.* At theater camp we collected Will Expressions, although mostly we were into insults."

She launched into a speech about how her friend

Henry kept lists of Will Expressions, but I didn't even pretend to listen. All I could think about was Gemma kissing Liam, Liam kissing Gemma—and wondering why that image made my insides knot up.

The first scene of *Romeo and Juliet* is long. There's a street fight, and then all the grown-ups appear, including the Prince, who yells at everybody to stop. Then Romeo's dad asks Benvolio what's been going on with Romeo, who's been acting weird lately. Benvolio says he doesn't know, Romeo's dad leaves, and Benvolio runs into Romeo, who says he's hopelessly in love with some girl (Rosaline, not Juliet). I guess because the scene goes on a while and has so many characters, Mr. Torres spent the first three rehearsals working on it. And since Paris only appears for a minute at the start of Scene Two, I didn't need to show up until Thursday.

In class, though, we were zooming along with the play, talking about the scene in Act One when Romeo and Juliet first meet at the costume party.

"Yeah, about that," Ajay said, not even bothering to raise his hand. "Isn't Romeo kind of a jerk for dumping Rosaline the second he meets Juliet?"

"He's not a jerk," I said. "He really *did* think he was in love with Rosaline. But he doesn't realize it's only a crush until he meets Juliet."

"What's so great about Juliet?" Ajay challenged me.

"I don't know," I admitted. "It can't just be that Romeo thinks she's pretty, because she's probably wearing a mask, right? And if she were really that amazing-looking, everybody in the play would be mentioning it all the time. And they don't. I think Romeo and Juliet just have a special connection."

"A special *connection*?" Ajay repeated, snorting.

"Because that's what love is," I said. "It doesn't need to make sense. It's like a chemical reaction. It just *happens*."

The class was staring at me. My face grew hot.

"What Mattie means," Tessa said loudly, "is that love is mysterious. Who knows why anyone falls in love. With anybody." She pointed her chin at Elijah.

Mr. Torres nodded. "Good point, humans. We shouldn't decide that just because Romeo instantly switches from Rosaline to Juliet at the costume party, his love for Juliet isn't real."

"But what's it *based* on?" Elijah demanded. "One conversation at a party?"

Ajay smirked. "Yeah, when Romeo first talks to Juliet, he just says he wants to kiss her. He doesn't say anything about love."

"Hmm." Mr. Torres smiled. "Interesting. When does it become love?"

"When they kiss?" Keisha guessed.

Willow raised her hand. "Mr. Torres, after they kiss, Juliet tells Romeo, 'You kiss by the book.' Does that mean she thinks he's a *bad* kisser? You know, like he's just following an instruction manual?"

"They had an instruction manual for how to kiss?" Liam joked. "Elijah, you should read it, bro."

Some boys sniggered. Elijah blushed.

I raised my hand again. "I think when Juliet tells Romeo he kisses 'by the book,' she just means he's good at it. But I don't think it's *why* she falls in love. I think she kisses him *because* she's in love."

"Okay, so here's what I don't get," Elijah said. He actually turned to face me for the first time since Willow's party. "Romeo walks into the party, he sees Juliet, she sees him, and boom, now they're supposedly in love? I know it's Shakespeare, but that's pretty lame."

"Ah," Mr. Torres said. "I see we have a skeptic in the room. You don't believe in romantic love, Elijah?"

"I don't know about *that*," Elijah said. "I just don't believe that Romeo and Juliet *are* in love. Not the way they think they are. Or the way they talk about it."

"Then you're missing the point of the whole play," I exploded. "Love is talking *about* love! Romeo and Juliet fall in love *by talking*!"

"Whoa, Shakespeare Nerdgirl," Ajay said.

"*Both* of you," Mr. Torres said, raising his eyebrows. "You know that's not how we communicate in this classroom."

"Sorry," Ajay and I muttered.

But I wasn't sorry. Not at all. Because if Elijah couldn't get this concept, then we had nothing in common, after all.

And therefore, *ping*. This was the moment I was officially out of crush.

If I was ever actually in crush to begin with.

15

"Madam, your mother craves
a word with you."
—*Romeo and Juliet*, I.v.113

At dismissal on Friday, Lucy asked if I wanted to get fro-yo. She'd had rehearsals every afternoon since Monday, and this was the first time we could hang out together all week. Tessa had left straight from school to spend the weekend with her dad, so it would be just the two of us— which sometimes felt more relaxing, to be honest.

"Sure," I said right away. I wasn't even nervous about being welcome at Verona's if Tessa wasn't coming. "But maybe we could stay and watch rehearsal first? Just for a bit?"

"What for?" Lucy asked.

"Well, it's Friday, so there's no homework or anything. And I wanted to see Gemma's first scene."

"Yeah, okay," she said, although without too much

enthusiasm. "Although you didn't stick around to see *my* first scene."

"You wanted me to? I thought you always hate it when people watch your dance rehearsals."

"I'm teasing, Mattie. Sure, we can watch for a few minutes. I bet Keisha would appreciate an audience."

Lucy and I walked into the auditorium and took seats in the second-to-last row. Right away, Lucy started texting somebody—Tessa, most likely—while I sat mesmerized by the scene. I'd forgotten that it was all about *me*: my character, Paris, had asked Lord Capulet for Juliet's hand (even though she was only thirteen). So in this scene, Juliet's mom was telling her about Paris's proposal, while the Nurse won't shut up about how cute Juliet was as a baby.

"What I don't understand," Gemma was telling Mr. Torres, "is why Juliet doesn't tell her mum to just sod off. She doesn't even *know* this Paris bloke. And she barely says a word in the whole scene."

"True, Juliet is being very quiet here," Mr. Torres said. "But look at what she does say to Lady Capulet: 'It is an honor that I dream not of.' That's not exactly *Yippee, I'm getting hitched.*"

"Yes, but then at the end of the scene she says she'll have a look at this Paris: 'But no more deep will I endart mine eye than your consent gives strength to make it fly.' What's she saying—*I'll check him out, but I won't do anything without your permission, Mummy*? She's being kind of wimpy about it, isn't she?"

"But she's just a kid," Keisha argued. "And in Shakespeare's time, what choice did she have? If your parents told you to marry someone, you did, right?" She looked at Mr. Torres.

"I'm afraid that *is* right," Mr. Torres said. "Juliet really was in no position to refuse. Or to rebel."

"Although she *does* rebel," Gemma insisted. "By falling in love with Romeo. But maybe in this scene she doesn't know yet that she has it in her."

"That she has *what* in her?" Mr. Torres asked, smiling.

"Bravery," Gemma said. "Not caring what anyone else thinks about her love."

"That's true," I murmured. "Gemma's really smart."

"Mm-hmm," Lucy said.

"Who's playing Paris again?" Charlotte was asking.

"Mattie," Keisha said.

"Well, at least Paris is pretty, then," Gemma said, laughing. "But I still hate Juliet's parents. They're treating their daughter as if she's a piece of property. All they care about is that this Paris bloke is rich."

Lucy poked me. "Let's go. I'm starving."

But I couldn't leave. Not if they were still discussing my character. And Gemma had just called me PRETTY.

"Five more minutes, okay?" I whispered, barely breathing.

Lucy sighed and twisted her hair.

But then Mr. Torres started working with Keisha on the Nurse's lines, while Gemma and Charlotte chatted together.

There was nothing to watch. So Lucy and I left the auditorium for fro-yo.

With Tessa gone for the weekend, Tessa's mom was probably bored, so on Saturday afternoon she called my mom to nag her about volunteering for some kind of PTA thing. Tessa's mom was the kind of person who wouldn't stop talking until you finally surrendered, and I knew Mom wasn't a big fan of her usual ranting. But I could hear Mom being polite to her on the phone, saying "yep," and "uh-huh," while she cleaned the kitchen counter.

When she finally hung up, Mom crossed her eyes. "So," she said. "Congratulate me. You're looking at the next eighth-grade Valentine's Dance committee chairperson."

"What's that?" I asked as I finished my tuna sandwich.

"The PTA needs a parent volunteer to organize things. And apparently I've just been recruited."

"Oh," I said. "Well, have fun with that."

"You sound as if you don't care one way or the other."

"I don't, honestly. I haven't even thought about the Valentine's Dance."

"Why not?"

"Because it's a million years from now! I'm much more focused on the play."

"I know you are, Mattie, and that's great," Mom said. "But the dance *isn't* a million years away; it's actually just a week after the play. And I know things didn't work out with that boy you liked—"

"Who?" I stared at her.

"That boy Lucy was talking about in the car, after the Halloween party. But as Grandma used to say, there are plenty of other fish in the sea."

Erg. "Mom, I'm totally over Elijah."

"Well, good." She tilted her head and smiled coyly. "Is there someone *else* you'd maybe like to go with?"

"To the dance? *No.*"

"So go with your friends! Plenty of kids won't have dates. It'll be fun, just a big dress-up party for the end of middle school. And I know Tessa's going."

Tessa would, I thought. A chance to wear something outrageous and dance with Liam Harrison. And probably Lucy will say she's going so she can Tessa-sit, but really, she'll be totally into it herself. Especially the dancing part.

"I'll think about it, okay?" I said.

"Okay," Mom said, giving up. "But if you decide yes, would you please let me know as soon as possible, so we'll have enough time to shop for a dress?"

"I don't need a dress," I said. "If I go, I'll just wear the Darth Vader costume."

She looked so horrified I had to explain that I was joking.

❀ 16 ❀

"O, then I see Queen Mab
hath been with you."
—*Romeo and Juliet*, I.iv.53

On Monday, I stayed for rehearsal mostly because of Lucy's comment that I hadn't been watching her scenes. I knew she'd been teasing when she'd said it, but I still felt a bit guilty that I hadn't stuck around for rehearsals last week—except for Friday, when Lucy wanted to do something else. So instead of sitting way in the back of the auditorium, the way we did on Friday, I sat in the third row, to make sure that Lucy could see me. And I wasn't even the only one in the audience! Keisha was there in the front row, sitting with Ellie Yamaguchi. Who both grinned and waved at me, like I hadn't just seen them the period before in science.

Today was a rehearsal for Act One Scene Four, which was Romeo, Benvolio, and Mercutio on the way to the Capulets' costume party. Romeo says he feels nervous about crashing the Capulets' party, and also too depressed about Rosaline to feel like dancing. Then he says he had a dream, and Mercutio teases him, giving a big speech about Queen Mab that I didn't understand at all.

I could tell by the way Tessa was reciting her lines that she didn't get it either. Usually Tessa was loud and dramatic, her arms and hands busy making gestures. But as she went on and on about Queen Mab and her wagon "tickling a parson's nose as he lies asleep," her voice was flat and her arms hung at her sides.

Finally, Mr. Torres stopped her.

"Tessa, what do you think Mercutio is saying here?" he asked.

"No idea," she admitted. "He just keeps talking! And I can't even breathe when I'm saying all these words."

"Oh, we'll work on the breathing, don't worry. But as for what he's going on about—"

Just then the auditorium door opened. In walked Willow, Charlotte, and Gemma.

I pretended to stare at the stage, and not to notice that Gemma had plopped into the seat on my left.

"Hullo," she whispered. The Gemma scent wafted off her, fresh and powdery. Not like perfume you'd buy at a makeup counter. Definitely not a mom smell.

"Hi," I said.

Willow and Charlotte took the two seats behind us. Right away, I could feel their eyes drilling holes into the back of my head.

My heart thumped.

"Basically, Mercutio is free-styling," Mr. Torres was telling Tessa. "Romeo says he had a dream, and Mercutio is kind of saying, *Yeah? You think YOU'RE the dreamy type? Mr. Romantic Poet, Mr. Imagination? Well, listen to THIS!* And then he's improvising what's almost a rap, showing off how imaginative *he* is."

Tessa's eyes lit up. "So it's like he's competing with Romeo? About who's the better poet?"

"Exactly," Mr. Torres said.

That was when Liam's friends Devlin, Noel, and Jamal took seats to our left. You could see Liam acknowledge them with his eyebrows. *The cool boy's greeting*, I thought.

Then Liam said, "Mr. Torres? Why is Mercutio making Romeo look stupid?"

"He isn't," Lucy said. "He's actually making Romeo look *normal*."

Tessa pretended she was insulted. "Are you saying Mercutio is crazy?"

"No," Lucy said, smiling. "Just that he overdoes everything, right? So compared to him, Romeo looks calm. And sane."

That was smart, I thought. Lucy was good at this.

"But who's Queen Mab?" Liam asked, flipping through his copy of the play. "She's not even in the cast list."

Gemma tugged on my sleeve, like she wanted me to lean toward her. So I did.

"Poor Liam," she whispered in my ear. "He's such a dim muppet, isn't he?"

I burst into giggles. *Dim muppet.* The thought of Liam with blue fur, talking like Grover, was too hilarious.

From the stage, everyone stared at me: Tessa, Lucy, Liam, and Mr. Torres.

"Mattie, are you all right?" Mr. Torres asked.

"Sorry," I said, forcing myself to swallow a giggle. It burned my throat.

"You're welcome to watch, but I do need to ask all audience members to be respectful of the actors," Mr. Torres said, frowning.

Charlotte poked my back. "Ooh, teacher not happy with teacher's pet," she said in a stupid baby voice.

"Sod off, Charlotte," Gemma said calmly. She leaned over to whisper again. "Sorry, Mattie. Didn't mean to get you in trouble."

"It's okay," I whispered back. "It was just that expression. Calling Liam a muppet—"

"It means 'idiot.' Fuzz for brains."

"Yeah, I guessed. But he isn't stupid. He's just showing off for his friends."

"Which *is* stupid," Gemma said. "I think friends should make you want to be *brilliant.*"

Now Willow was the one poking my back. "Hey," she said. "Quiet, you guys. Don't make Mr. Torres mad at us."

"We won't," Gemma promised, winking at me.

We, I thought. She'd said it again.

The walk home with Tessa and Lucy was tense. I could tell that Tessa was still frustrated with the Queen Mab speech, even though now she understood why Mercutio was saying it. And Lucy wasn't talking, just twisting her hair and looking at the pavement.

"Are you mad at me?" I blurted.

Lucy opened her eyes wide. "Why would I be?"

"For laughing during rehearsal. I'm really sorry. It was just that Gemma said—"

"Yeah," Tessa cut in. "That *was* kind of weird. The way you were sitting with Willow and her Willow-ettes."

"*They* sat next to *me*," I protested. "And they kept poking me in the back. Oh, but good news: Gemma thinks Liam is dumb. She called him a *dim muppet!*"

Lucy seemed confused. "Why is that good news, Mattie?"

"Oh, because Tessa—"

Tessa's eyes said, *SHUT UP, MATTIE. LET'S NOT EMBARRASS ME, OKAY?*

So she hadn't told Lucy I was supposed to find out Gemma's opinion of Liam? That was surprising.

"I just thought Tessa would like that expression," I babbled. "Because of how she collects expressions. From Shakespeare, anyway. I guess people say it in England. Isn't it hilarious?"

"It's funny," Lucy said. "I guess."

But she seemed like she wasn't even listening, so I let it drop.

When I got home, my brothers were in the kitchen, eating potato chips.

"You can't come in here; it's base," Kayden informed me.

"Affirmative," I replied. "But I need to requisition edible supplies."

"For who?" he asked suspiciously. "The Jedi Counsel?"

"Sure. Them." I grabbed a handful of chips. "Is Mom home?"

Mason nodded. "Yeah, but she's in her office, and she said not to bother her. She said we didn't have to start our homework until four thirty. So you're invading our *game*, Mattie."

I bowed. "Then I shall retreat. Carry on, officers."

I had no idea whose side I was supposed to be on in this never-ending *Star Wars* game my little brothers were playing. But as long as it kept them relatively quiet and downstairs, I could stay in my room and just listen for crashes and screams and other signs of disaster. I didn't have to actually, literally *watch* them while Mom was working.

I flopped on my bed. Then I crocheted for a few minutes. Making cute little animals called *amigurumi* always calmed me. As soon as I'd finished my blue dolphin, I texted Tessa:

What happened before?

Immediately she answered : *yeah I know. Lucy*

I waited for ten entire minutes, but Tessa didn't add any information.

Lucy WHAT?? I wrote back.

sorry, Mom yelling. I think Lucy has a thing about Gemma.

What sort of a thing??

dunno. she was acting weird after you and Gemma were laughing.

Maybe she was just mad at me for being rude?

yeah that didn't help :P but she does have a Gemma thing?? I think??

Okay, but WHY do you think it??

just an impression lately. and when I asked her about it she wouldn't talk. maybe she's jealous?

About what?

Tessa didn't answer.

I waited ten more minutes.

Still no answer.

My heart was pounding as I texted: *Tessa? You there?*

yeah sorry.

Why would Lucy be jealous?

maybe she thinks you're in love with Gemma or something haha.

tessa, that's not funny!!!

sorry Mom yelling again bye

I couldn't believe Tessa was saying this. Lucy was the most sensible, logical, sane person I knew. She was nice *to* everybody and *about* everybody—even annoying people like Charlotte and Ajay. The whole time I'd known her—more than six years—she was never the least bit jealous or possessive. When Tessa went off with her theater camp friends, she was always happy for Tessa. And there was nothing to be jealous about, anyway: I'd had a few quick conversations with Gemma. That was IT. Not to mention the fact that Gemma was Willow's friend, and there was no way Willow would let me get any closer.

Plus, Tessa shouldn't have joked just now about me being in love with Gemma. I knew she didn't mean anything by it, but you didn't make jokes like that. Especially not at school, where if someone overheard and got the wrong idea, things could turn weird.

17

"Tell me in sadness,
who is that you love?"
—*Romeo and Juliet*, I.i.202

Tuesday's rehearsal was a big one—the costume party scene, when Romeo and Juliet first meet. Mercutio wasn't in it, weirdly enough, even though he says the Queen Mab speech on the way to the party. (Did Shakespeare just lose track? I liked thinking that even a megagenius like him could be spacey about his characters sometimes.) But at the end of English class, Mr. Torres convinced Tessa to hang out after dismissal anyway, to practice the Queen Mab speech with Miss Bluestone.

"Erg," Tessa muttered to me. "She'll probably spend the whole time talking about how she once went to Chipotle with Queen Mab."

I laughed. Then I asked Tessa if Lucy had said anything to her about the weirdness walking home yesterday.

"Nope," Tessa said. "Mattie, if you want to know, why don't you ask her yourself?"

But I couldn't. Even though whatever it was that was bothering Lucy yesterday was still going on today, apparently. At lunch, she was unusually quiet, explaining that she was just nervous about a math test. The thing was, Lucy was never nervous about tests. She studied hard and mostly aced them.

So I decided to go to rehearsal, even though Paris wasn't invited to the costume party. Maybe if I walked home afterward with Lucy, I could finally ask her about this "Gemma thing." Besides, I wanted to watch Gemma rehearse.

I sat myself in the second row of the auditorium, determined to be perfectly behaved this time. Gemma, of course, was onstage in this scene, so she couldn't make me giggle. Although she did wave at me from the stage, which made me smile.

"Okay, let's get started, humans," Mr. Torres was telling the cast. "This scene is one of the most important in the play and, along with the balcony scene that follows, one of the most famous in English literature. I want us to convey two different speeds: the hubbub of the party versus the actual encounter between Romeo and Juliet, which should have a time-standing-still quality."

"What do you mean?" Keisha asked.

"I mean, look at how Lord Capulet speaks as his servants are setting up the party and guests are arriving. Ajay, any thoughts?"

Ajay read his script. "It's like he's having three conversations at once."

Mr. Torres nodded. "Exactly. Lord Capulet can barely finish his sentences, and he keeps interrupting himself to talk with his guests and to give instructions to the servants. His speech is rapid and hectic, nothing fancy or figurative, right? And when Tybalt recognizes Romeo through his costume, how does he speak, Willow?"

"He tells Lord Capulet to expose Romeo and kick him out," Willow said. "Tybalt just comes out and says it: ''Tis he, that villain Romeo.' And when Lord Capulet tells him to shut up, he just says, 'Why, uncle, 'tis a shame.' It's so simple; it doesn't even sound like Shakespeare."

"Brava, Willow," Mr. Torres said, beaming. "Tybalt is a young man of action, not words. Now look at how Romeo speaks when he sees Juliet."

"Yeah, about that," Liam said. "How come every time Romeo talks it stops making sense?" He glanced at the audience; I turned around and spotted some of his sporty friends, Noel, Devlin, and Jamal, sitting in the back.

What are they doing here? I wondered.

I could see Mr. Torres take a breath. "What doesn't make sense to you, Liam?"

"The whole thing. Like all this stuff he says about hands and lips and pilgrims. What do the Pilgrims have to do with it?" He grinned, peeking at his friends.

Gemma held the script in front of her face. I could see by the way her body was shaking that she was giggling.

"It's not about the Mayflower Pilgrims," Mr. Torres said evenly. "Romeo is comparing his own lips to 'two blushing pilgrims.'"

"Isn't that kind of gay?" Ajay said, sniggering.

Mr. Torres turned to him. "Ajay," he said, slowly and firmly. "People may choose to identify themselves as gay, and it's a word of pride. But the way *you're* using the word, it's just an insult, and there's no room for that in this production, or in this school. Understood?"

"Sorry," Ajay muttered. His head drooped.

"Yeah, Ajay," Willow said in her team-captain voice. "Nobody thinks that's funny. And even if Romeo *were* gay, which he isn't, so what?"

"Although *that* wouldn't make any sense," Keisha said. "Because Romeo loves Juliet, not Mercutio, right?"

"Yes, I think we can all agree on that." Mr. Torres smiled. "Tell you what. Why don't we start working on the beginning of the scene, and when we get to the part when Romeo sees Juliet, we'll talk some more, Liam."

Liam tossed his beautiful blond hair. "Yeah, whatever," he said.

I watched as Mr. Torres showed the kids playing the servants how to keep moving across the stage, doing party setup work as Lord Capulet moves in the opposite direction, crossing the stage to greet Tybalt. I hated to admit it, but I thought Ajay spoke his lines really well—not just confidently, but as if he got Lord Capulet's charming, obnoxious personality. And Willow as Tybalt was perfect: Her voice was loud, and she had the kind of athlete's energy that made you believe she could even be dangerous.

"The important thing is to keep moving," Mr. Torres was saying. "Notice all the times—and not just in this scene—the characters tell each other to hurry up, make haste. No one in this world has any time to *think*."

Finally, though, it was time for Romeo to notice Juliet. Mr. Torres told all the other actors to freeze in their positions. Then Liam began reading:

> "O, she doth teach the torches to burn bright!
> It seems she hangs upon the cheek of night
> As a rich jewel—"

Suddenly, he stopped. "Okay," he said, frowning. "I get that Shakespeare is trying to say that Juliet is sparkly? But I don't get this stuff about hanging on the cheek of night. So is Shakespeare, I mean Romeo, saying that Juliet is hanging on the cheek of night like she's a cheek piercing, or something?"

"No," Mr. Torres answered.

"Then what's she doing hanging on the cheek of night?" Now he was grinning at his friends in the audience.

Ajay was sniggering again.

"Liam, we'll talk about it, I promise," Mr. Torres said. "But for now, why don't you just say the words? We'll work on the meaning afterward."

I glanced at Gemma, who was crossing her eyes at me.

"Okay, and now Juliet," Mr. Torres said.

"Question," Gemma said. "Am I wearing a mask over my entire face? Because how will we kiss, then?"

"No, just over your eyes," Mr. Torres answered. He seemed a bit frazzled, I thought. "But we'll worry about costumes later. Yes, Liam?"

"So here's another question," Liam said. "If Romeo, like, wants to kiss Juliet, why does he talk about saints and pilgrims? Wouldn't she *not* want to kiss him if he's being so religious and everything?"

"That's kind of the joke," Gemma said. "But it also works, doesn't it? Because she lets him kiss her."

Liam stared at his book. "Yeah, it says 'kisses her' in the script."

"So come on, kiss her, man," Ajay taunted. "Kiss her, Liam."

"We're just *rehearsing* this scene, you prat," Gemma said.

Ajay pointed at the page. "Hey, it says 'kisses her' *twice*! You can't get out of this, Liam!"

"Right, then," Gemma said. She marched over to Liam and smooched him on the lips. "Are you happy now, Ajay?"

Liam practically toppled over. His friends in the audience cheered. Ajay gaped.

Keisha laughed, Willow frowned, and Lucy stared at me.

I swallowed. Why was Lucy staring at me?

"All right, folks, so now that we've gotten *that* out of the way, let's block the scene," Mr. Torres said.

"Block?" Keisha asked.

"That just means figure out where everyone stands," Mr. Torres explained quickly. "Gemma and Liam, lines, please."

As they spoke, Gemma and Liam touched hands, like they were one person praying. Liam, who'd obviously been shaken by Gemma's kiss, practically whispered his lines, but Gemma's voice was clear and full of wonder. Almost as if she were saying: *I've never touched a boy's hands before, or even stood this close to one. This is incredible.* And you could tell she had no trouble with the meaning.

Still, it was hard for me to watch. Just the thought of Gemma's hands pressed against Liam's seemed so wrong, and I couldn't bear the thought of his stupid, conceited hand germs mixing with hers. In a way, this hand pressing was worse than the kiss. Because the kiss had been a joke. And unlike the hand pressing, it was over fast.

My chest felt tight, as if it had shrunk somehow and now my lungs didn't have enough space. *Breathe,* I told myself. *Breathe again.*

When I looked up, I saw Lucy still watching me from the stage. I waved; she nodded.

"Nice," Mr. Torres was saying. "The rest of this scene needs to happen chaotically, in fast motion, so let's see plenty of energy, okay?" He showed Lucy where to stand for her one line telling Romeo to leave the party. Then he showed Keisha where to be as she told Juliet the identity of the boy she'd kissed.

"Thanks, humans," Mr. Torres said. "Great job today. Liam, can I see you for a few minutes?"

While Gemma, Keisha, and Willow were laughing together, I waited for Lucy to jump off the stage.

"Good rehearsal," I told her.

She grunted. "I can't believe I had to give up an entire afternoon for just one line. Benvolio does *nothing* this scene!"

"At least you're in it," I said. "Paris doesn't show up again until Act Three. You want to walk home?"

"Sure." Lucy gathered her jacket and her backpack, not saying anything to anyone else, including me.

We left the auditorium together. It was the second week of November, and the wind was icy sharp. I buttoned the top button of my jacket, wishing I'd worn the scarf I'd crocheted last winter. The good news was that I'd stuffed my red mittens into my pockets, and they were still wearable, even though both thumbs had nickel-size holes.

"So what do you think?" I said, because Lucy wasn't talking. "Is Liam going to ruin the play?"

"I hope not," Lucy said. "Why did Mr. Torres cast him, anyway?"

"No idea. But hardly any boys came to tryouts, and he wanted someone from our class to play Romeo, so . . ."

"Well, he's a disaster. Did you see the way he kept looking at his friends in the audience? It's like he was goofing for *them*."

"Yeah," I said. "Maybe he's embarrassed about being Romeo."

"Then he shouldn't have tried out with Romeo's speech, right?"

"I guess," I said. "Although he probably hadn't read the play before tryouts. Maybe he didn't realize what he was getting into."

"Then Mr. Torres should've explained it to him. Before it was too late to do anything about it."

We walked another block. I waited for her to say something else on the subject of Liam, but she didn't. She didn't even make mindless small talk. So obviously, if there was going to be any conversation at all, I needed to be the one to make it happen.

"Anyway," I said brightly. "At least Gemma's great. Don't you think so?"

Lucy looked at me. "Gemma?"

"I mean as Juliet. Don't you think she says her lines really well? And with so much expression?"

"Uh-huh."

I took a deep breath. "Lucy? Can I ask you—is something wrong? I mean, about Gemma?"

"*Not at all*," Lucy said emphatically. She stopped walking, and looked straight into my eyes. "Mattie, really, I'm totally okay with it. I just didn't *know* before."

"Know what?"

"The whole thing. How you felt."

"About what?"

It was like Mr. Torres said: Some scenes go fast. Some seem to stop time.

This was a time stopper.

"About *what*?" My heart was picking up speed. "Lucy, what are you talking about?"

"Mattie, it's fine," Lucy said. "I won't tell anyone if you don't want. Not even Tessa."

"Tell her what?"

"How you feel about Gemma. That you're in love, or have a crush on her, or whatever."

"*What?*" I shook my head. I couldn't speak.

This wasn't a joke. She really meant it.

"Oh, Mattie, come on, it's obvious," Lucy said quietly. "The way you talk to her. The way you talk *about* her."

My head was shaking. My whole body was shaking.

"The look on your face when she kissed Liam just now. I was thinking *something* was going on, because you've been so weird lately—keeping secrets from us, not dealing with Elijah. And the way you freaked out at Willow's party—"

"Lucy, what does the *party* have to do with—"

"I didn't know, until you mentioned that you'd been hanging with *Gemma* in the kitchen. So that's why you were so embarrassed about being discovered, right? Anyway, I had a feeling about you and Gemma. And today at the rehearsal, I just . . . was sure."

"No," I said hoarsely. "Lucy, listen to me, okay? You're totally wrong about Gemma. And me."

She shrugged. "Okay."

"I mean, yes, I like her, I like her *a lot*, but I don't—"

"It's *fine* with me, Mattie. I'm still your best friend. I just don't like secrets."

"Lucy," I said helplessly. "Nothing is going on."

"Okay, Mattie. I said *okay*." All of a sudden, she threw her arms around me and squeezed. "We won't talk about it if you don't want to."

Then she ran down the street to her house.

18

"O, she doth teach the torches
to burn bright!"
—*Romeo and Juliet*, I.v. 46

I zombie-walked home.

My little brothers were racing around the living room in their Stormtrooper costumes. And I did a demented thing: I asked if I could play with them. They were both shocked, because I only ever played with them as a bribe. But that day, I actually *wanted* to put on the Darth Vader costume, be covered from head to toe, talk into a voice-changer thingy. And especially to have lines to say, already written and pre-acted. Because I didn't want to have to think. I didn't even want to improvise. *The force is strong with this one. I am your father. You don't know the power of the Dark Side.*

"I really appreciate this, Mattie," Mom said as she called us into supper. "I was on the computer all afternoon with a work deadline."

"Any time," I lied.

After supper, which I could barely swallow, I started my math homework. But I couldn't focus.

Because: *OMIGOD. Is Lucy right? Can I possibly have a crush on Gemma Braithwaite?*

I really liked her. Really, really, in fact.

Yes, but WHY?

Because she was smart. And funny. And pretty.

Although pretty wasn't relevant. Not to friendship, right? I wasn't friends with Tessa and Lucy because of pretty. So why did pretty matter with Gemma Braithwaite?

It shouldn't. It didn't.

Okay, fine. Why *else* did I like her?

That accent.

But it was more than the accent—it was her voice. Whispery but clear and strong.

Also, I liked that she liked words. She liked saying them: remember all those *t* sounds in her tryout? And she liked expressions, the same way I did. *DIM MUPPET. DANG.*

And the way she said her lines: It was like Shakespeare had written the words just for her.

Of course he hadn't, but seriously, she was super talented.

Yeah, but Tessa was talented too. Even Ajay said his lines incredibly well. So did Willow, for that matter. So it definitely wasn't just about talent.

Then what was it I liked about Gemma Braithwaite?
I thought.
I liked the way she wanted to be friends, despite Willow.
I liked the way she wasn't shy about kissing Liam.
I liked her braid, the way it fell over her shoulder.
I liked the pink streak in her hair at tryouts.
The way her eyelashes were wet on the balcony.
The way she smelled like Gemma powder.
The way she crossed her eyes at me onstage.
The way she leaned over my rehearsal calendar.
The way she dueled me with the straw.
The way she laughed.
The way she called us *we*.

All right, I told myself. But even if you felt all those things, if you added them up, did it equal a crush?

And if it did—not that I was saying it *was* a crush, just saying *IF*—would it mean that you were gay, or a lesbian, or whatever word you were supposed to call it, if you liked only one particular girl?

Who wasn't just *any* girl, but the Star of Our Show, the perfect choice for Juliet, pirate treasure?

Who, let's face it, *everybody* liked. Because the weird thing would be *not* to have a crush on Gemma Braithwaite.

Or were you just—I mean, *was I*—overthinking again?

19

"Had I it written, I would tear the word."
—*Romeo and Juliet*, II.ii.57

I hardly ever ran into Gemma at school, but the next day, she was everywhere. I saw her in the halls. In the lunchroom. In the PE bathroom. And every time I saw her braid or heard her laugh or her whispery voice, my heart zoomed. All day it felt as if I'd been set at the wrong speed, and would end up crashing into a wall or something. But I still kept looking for her, seeing her, and then asking myself: *Is it happening again? Am I zooming?*

And I was. Every time.

I couldn't deny it.

Whatever it meant about me.

Once she even waved at me across the hall and called out, "Hullo, Mattie." Pronouncing the *t*s in my name as if she were cutting them out in little stars.

"Hey," I said back. At that moment my head felt so strange and swimmy that I could barely remember her name. And when I finally did, it was too late to add it to the *Hey*. So I just waved back. And kept walking.

Wednesday was a short rehearsal because it was a short scene—Mercutio and Benvolio searching for Romeo after he runs out of the party. I considered not going that afternoon, just coming straight home to do the homework I'd blown off the day before. Maybe washing my hair again, even though it was clean. But I knew that if I avoided rehearsal, Lucy would think I was avoiding *her*. And the only thing I could think of doing was nothing—acting as if everything was the same as always, as if we hadn't even had that conversation.

Plus, I wanted to know if Lucy had said anything to Tessa about the Gemma-and-me situation. Although I suspected by Tessa's behavior that the answer was no. Tessa was a good actress, but she was the worst secret keeper in the world, incapable of not blabbing things immediately. So I felt pretty positive that if she knew what Lucy had said to me, and how I'd answered Lucy, she would have jumped on this topic like it was a bouncy castle.

Instead, she ranted about how Miss Bluestone did nothing to help her with the Queen Mab speech. The whole time they were supposed to be rehearsing, Tessa said, Miss Blue-

stone just reminisced about the "glorious" Shakespeare productions she saw "in her youth." So Lucy suggested going to
Mrs. Dimona for help, but Tessa wouldn't even consider it;
she was convinced Mrs. Dimona had hated her ever since
sixth grade, when Tessa's mom backed into Mrs. Dimona's
minivan in the school parking lot, resulting in a small cra-
ter in Mrs. Dimona's fender and plenty of ranting (for once,
not about politics) from Tessa's mom.

"What about asking Mr. Torres?" I suggested as the
three of us walked home that afternoon.

"Yeah, I would," Tessa said, "except he's so busy working with Liam."

Lucy was eyeing me. "Mattie has some extra time," she
said. "Maybe she could help you."

"Oh, that would be awesome-tacular," Tessa shouted.
"Would you, Mattie? Pleeease?" She did the begging thing
with her hands.

"Okay," I said, "but that speech is super difficult. Truthfully, I'm not sure I get it."

"You probably get it better than I do! Anyway, I really
just need someone to listen to me say it like fifteen times in
a row. And we still have tons of leftover Halloween candy
at my house."

"Sure," I said. "This weekend. But Lucy has to come
too."

"We'll have a three-way rehearsal-slash-candy binge," Lucy said, smiling.

Tessa threw her arms around Lucy and me. "I looove my friends," she shouted to the sky. "I loooove them!"

And I wondered: Would she have said *love* if she knew?

Next day was the famous balcony scene, when Juliet says, "Romeo, Romeo, wherefore art thou Romeo?" and "A rose by any other name would smell as sweet." Oh, and also "Parting is such sweet sorrow." The good news was that all of those lines, which were like Shakespeare's Greatest Hits, would be said by Gemma, so I didn't have to worry that Liam would ruin them. Still, I wasn't planning on showing up at rehearsal after school. I wasn't sure I could stand watching. And I wasn't sure I could be in the same auditorium as Gemma.

But then Tessa grabbed me at the lockers at dismissal. "You're going today, right?"

We were at the point where if one of us said *going*, the other one didn't need to ask where. I started to tell Tessa I was skipping rehearsal, but she insisted I needed to go. Panicking, I asked her why.

"Because it's *That Scene*," she explained. "I want to check out Liam, but it would look creepy if I went by myself. So you *have* to come, Mattie. Lucy, too."

I couldn't think up a decent excuse fast enough, so I just said okay. A minute later, Lucy showed up and said okay also. She smiled at me in a supportive way, but I pretended not to notice.

Five minutes later the three of us took seats in the third row of the auditorium. Dead center.

Mr. Torres was chatting with Liam in the corner of the stage. Gemma was shuffling her feet and swaying center stage, listening to something through earbuds, when she suddenly saw us.

"Mattie!" she called, yanking out the earbuds and jumping off the stage.

My heart thumped as she ran over to us, grinning.

"Hullo, Tessa and Lucy! Are you staying for the whole rehearsal today? I'm so nervous I think I might throw up."

"I'm sure you won't," I said, willing myself not to blush.

"Mattie, you're so sweet." Gemma leaned toward me, her braid coming close to my cheek. "Although I'm starting to worry about Liam. I think *he's* starting to worry as well. Mr. Torres is giving him a pep talk. Don't look."

Of course Tessa looked. "I don't like his body language," she commented. "He looks floppy."

"Yes, he said something about being exhausted from ice hockey practice. Apparently, they have to be at the rink at some hideous hour—five in the morning, I think. Can you imagine that?" She shuddered. "But I think the real problem is—Ooh, look, there's Willow. Hullo, Willow! And Charlotte and Isabel! Excuse me."

She hurried over to chat with her friends. For a second I wondered if Willow had come to watch Gemma or Liam. I mean, if she had to choose. Which, of course, she didn't.

Also, I noticed Liam's friends gathered in the back of the auditorium. Noel, Devlin, Jamal, and a seventh grader named Max this time, too.

"Can we get started, please," Mr. Torres was saying. "I see we have an audience today. I hope I don't need to tell you that this scene requires the full focus of the actors, so if there's any distraction, I'll ask you to leave. Got it?"

"No problem, Mr. Torres," Willow sang out.

"Good. Okay, Act Two, Scene Two. Capulet's orchard. First Romeo speaks, then Juliet appears at the window. Romeo, line, please?"

"He jests at scars that never felt a wound," Liam recited. "Mr. Torres, that doesn't make sense."

Mr. Torres smiled cheerfully. "Well, Benvolio and Mercutio had just been making fun of Romeo's lovesickness. Although they both still think Romeo is pining for Rosaline, right? Romeo overhears them, and basically he's saying they don't know what they're talking about, because they've never been in love."

Liam tossed his hair. "So why does Romeo say *he*? Shouldn't he say *they*?"

"Yes, but it's like a saying: *He who laughs last laughs best. He who hesitates is lost.* 'He who' just means 'a person,' okay? Anyway, now Juliet appears at the window. Juliet, please stand on this riser. Romeo, you're here, looking up at her." Mr. Torres put his hands on Liam's shoulders and turned him toward Gemma.

"This is stupid," Liam said. "I'm supposed to be saying all this stuff, and she won't hear it?" He glanced at his friends in the audience.

"When we build the scenery it'll be more plausible," Mr. Torres said. "For now, pretend there's an orchard wall behind you, and you're standing at Juliet's open window, which is on the first floor. All right? Please begin."

Liam started reading the speech that begins, "But soft! What light through yonder window breaks? It is the east, and Juliet is the sun!" I think it was Romeo's longest speech so far, maybe in the whole play, and as he was saying the words, you could tell that Liam's mind was starting to wander, especially when Jamal and Devlin started laughing about something.

Then Liam said:

"It is my lady; O, it is my love!

O, that she knew she were!

She speaks, yet she says nothing. What of that?

Her eye discourses; I will answer it.

I am too bold; 'tis not to me she speaks.

Two of the fairest stars in all the heaven,

Having some business, do entreat her eyes

To twinkle in their spheres till they return.

What if her eyes were there, they in her head?"

"Hey," Liam said, looking up from his script. "Can I ask something? I get that Romeo is saying Juliet's eye is talking, which is kind of weird, right? But then he says that there are these two stars that have, like, an errand to go on, right? And so Juliet's eyeballs should go up in the sky for the stars until they get back? So it's like an eyeballs-for-stars swap? That's kind of funny, man." He grinned at his friends.

Gemma's eye caught mine. Her cheeks were pink, and I could see she was desperately fighting off giggles. Pee-in-your-pants giggles. I bit the insides of my cheeks and stared at my uneven fingernails.

"I agree," Mr. Torres was saying patiently. "It *is* a little funny, Liam. But let's keep going, okay?"

"WOO, LIAM," Isabel called out. "YOU GOT THIS, BRO."

Mr. Torres glared at her. "Isabel, this isn't a football

game, and we don't need cheerleading. I said if you were noisy I'd ask you to leave, and I meant it."

"She'll shut up," Willow said. "I promise."

"Another peep, and you're *all* gone, humans. I'm serious. And that goes for the newcomers, too." Mr. Torres pointed to the far left of the auditorium, where Ajay, Keisha, Jake, and some other kids were now sitting. Then he glared at Liam's friends in the back row, who were moving around restlessly. One of them—Devlin—was even standing, pretending to shoot invisible basketballs at an invisible hoop. "All right, Liam, let's take it from *What if her eyes were there?*"

Liam read his lines as if he had a blob of extra-chunky peanut butter on his tongue. Next it was Gemma's turn to say, "O Romeo, Romeo, wherefore art thou Romeo? Deny thy father and refuse thy name."

"What's Montague? it is nor hand, nor foot,
Nor arm, nor face, nor any other part
Belonging to a man. O, be some other name!
What's in a name! That which we call a rose
By any other name would smell as sweet;
So Romeo would, were he not Romeo call'd—"

"Wait," Liam interrupted. "The problem is his *last* name,

right? Not his first. So why does she tell him to not be Romeo? Shouldn't she say not to be *Montague*?"

Good point, actually, I thought.

"She's just saying names don't matter," Mr. Torres said. "Any names. Try not to overthink this, Liam."

"Heh," Lucy murmured. "I don't think overthinking is Liam's problem."

"Not funny," Tessa said.

"You guys, quiet; he'll kick us out," I whispered. *Although that might not be so bad*, I told myself, as I watched Liam's friends finally leave the auditorium.

Now Juliet was asking Romeo, "Art thou not Romeo, and a Montague?"

> Romeo: "Neither, fair maid, if either thee dislike."
> Juliet: "How camest thou hither, tell me, and wherefore?
> The orchard walls are high and hard to climb,
> And the place death, considering who thou art,
> If any of my kinsmen find thee here."
> Romeo: "With love's light wings did I o'er-perch these walls;
> For stony limits cannot hold love out,

And what love can do, that dares love attempt;
Therefore thy kinsmen"—*Aw, forget it, man.*

We watched in shock as Liam flung his script across the stage.

"Hey!" Mr. Torres looked stunned. "What's the problem, Liam? I thought you were doing very well there."

"Nah. This play sucks, man. It's just all these *words*."

"Well, sure," Gemma said. "Don't forget, I'm saying them too."

"Yeah, but you make them *sound* right. I'm just—" He shook his head helplessly.

"Poor Liam," Tessa murmured.

"Why don't we talk through the lines, like we did after rehearsal yesterday?" Mr. Torres said. "Juliet is asking Romeo how he got there, right? And remember, 'wherefore' means 'why.' So she's asking him why he came back to her house. Then she says, 'The orchard walls are high and hard to climb,'—"

"That's what I mean," Liam exploded. "I can't *do* this Shakespeare stuff."

Mr. Torres took a deep breath. "Please help me understand the problem, Liam, okay? Are you not getting what Juliet's saying here? Because it's pretty direct. I think if you focus—"

Liam shrugged. I could tell that his brain had left the auditorium when his friends walked out. Probably he just wanted to hang with them, shoot baskets, forget this whole Romeo business.

"Okay, look," Mr. Torres said. "When she says, 'The orchard walls are high and hard to climb,' it means—"

"The orchard walls are high and hard to climb," Ajay yelled out.

Somebody guffawed.

"Shut up, Ajay," Willow shouted. "That isn't funny."

Mr. Torres spun around and glared at the audience. "Okay, everybody out!"

"But that's not fair," Tessa blurted. "Why should *we* be kicked out just because of Willow?"

"Because of *me*, Tessa?" Willow snapped. "You mean because of Ajay! *He's* the one who—"

"Because *none* of you are behaving like mature eighth graders!" Mr. Torres snapped, sounding exactly like Possibly Verona. "What's the deal here today, people? You think this is easy? Or that maybe *you* can do a better job? Is that it? You want to be Romeo, Ajay?"

Ajay turned purple. "No, Mr. Torres. Sorry. I didn't mean—"

"Leave, all of you! *Now*. And no more audiences at rehearsals until I say so. Which I may never do, if I can't count on you to behave appropriately." He turned. I could see his back rising and falling in a sharp, frustrated sigh. "Okay, Liam. Let's just take a minute and then we'll go through this word by word."

20

"But I pray, can you read any thing you see?"
"Ay, if I know the letters and the language."
—*Romeo and Juliet*, I.ii. 60–61

It's a funny thing. I've seen my parents annoyed with my sister, Cara, and with my brothers, and once in a while even with me. But I never worried. I always knew that no matter how angry they felt, they'd get over it eventually.

But when Mr. Torres yelled and kicked us out of rehearsal, I felt like crying.

Not only because I hated to think my favorite teacher was mad at me—even though he wasn't mad at me personally. Just mad at all of us.

And not only because I could see the production was in bad trouble.

But also because, by the way Gemma had greeted me—greeted all of us, really—I could tell that she actually *liked* having people in the audience. So the whole thing seemed extra unfair, because if Liam's concentration was the problem, why did Gemma have to suffer? And why did the rest of us, too?

But, of course, I couldn't say anything to Mr. Torres. Especially the Gemma part—there was no way I could express Gemma's feelings for her. I mean, if I even knew her feelings, anyway.

The next morning, my homeroom teacher, Ms. Crenshaw, said that Mr. Torres had asked to see me as soon as I got there. She frowned at me, as if the fact I was in trouble was perfectly obvious to her.

"What's going on?" Tessa asked as I gathered my backpack and jacket.

"Not sure," I mumbled. "I'm being summoned."

"Better not betray your co-conspirators, Monaghan. Or we'll come after you in the dark of night."

"Mum's the word."

I walked upstairs to the second floor. Mr. Torres didn't have his own homeroom, so his classroom was empty. As soon as he saw me standing at the door, he jumped up from his desk to close the door behind me.

He seemed a bit jittery, I thought. Also, as if he needed a shave. And probably a better night's sleep, too: He had shadows under his eyes.

"Thanks for coming," he said.

You sent for me; why are you thanking me?

"Um, sorry about yesterday," I said. "I know we were distracting."

"Not your fault, Mattie. And sorry I blew up like that. It was a long day, and a challenging rehearsal." He drank some coffee from a mug that had that Christmas-present-from-a-student look: the head of an author-type male (Charles Dickens?) with a handle. Although why anyone, even a teacher, would want to drink out of a famous author's *open head* was kind of a mystery.

"Would you like a cookie? My wife made some for the cast." Mr. Torres went over to his closet to get a Tupperware, took off the lid, and passed the whole container to me. Chocolate chip. Maybe they were apology cookies for kicking us out yesterday.

"They look great," I said. "Thanks. But I just had breakfast, so . . ."

"Take one for later," he urged me. "They'll disappear by rehearsal. And you're not scheduled for today, right?"

"Right." He had to know that Paris wasn't in today's scene. What was going on here?

"Thanks," I said again. I took a cookie and put it on top of my backpack, which was at my feet. Then I looked up at him, waiting for him to explain what I was doing there.

"So, Mattie," he finally said. "I'd like to chat with you about a special project. I'm sure you noticed at rehearsal yesterday that one of our actors has lost a bit of confidence."

"You mean Liam?"

Mr. Torres nodded reluctantly, as if he hadn't wanted to name anybody in particular. "He's struggling with the part, questioning everything. Despite his joking around, he's a bright, hardworking student, so I know he *can* get the role, but the more I try to help him—well, it's just not happening. I think what he needs at this point is to read the lines with a peer. Another student, not a teacher. In a friendly, casual, low-pressure sort of way."

"You want me to help Liam?"

"Exactly. I have a lot of faith in your ability to do this, Mattie. You're a terrific reader, and you've read the entire play on your own, right?"

"Yes," I admitted. "But I didn't understand every word!"

"That isn't necessary. Just do your best to help him make sense of what he's saying, and if you have a question about anything, I'm here to help."

I swallowed. "But couldn't Miss Bluestone or Mrs. Dimona work with Liam? I've never tutored before, or whatever."

Mr. Torres caught my eye. "They could," he answered carefully. "Although I'm convinced they're not what Liam needs right now. He needs to relax, and I think he's the type of student who relaxes most when he's with his peers."

"But when would we do this?" I asked, my mind starting to race. "He has rehearsal almost every day. And I think he plays ice hockey too, doesn't he?"

"Yes, that's right. He's way overscheduled, which is a big reason why he's so stressed. So I'm asking you to meet with him during English class. I've gotten permission for you two to use the stage that period."

"You mean I'll be missing English? Every *day*?"

"Don't worry, I'll keep you posted on what we do. Fortunately, Paris is a small part, so you won't have too many lines of your own to work on. Oh, and another thing: I'm also going to ask you to come to rehearsals, so you can see what's working, and what needs a little extra attention. But just you, Mattie—nobody else. I think allowing open rehearsals was part of the problem; he was distracted by his friends, and too many people in the audience made Liam nervous."

I almost said: *But he's going to be performing in front of the* entire school *in a few weeks, plus people's parents and grandparents. So if he's nervous in front of a few classmates, how is he supposed to deal with opening night?*

But all of a sudden, then, the whole thing came into focus for me. Tutoring Romeo was going to be torture, no doubt about it—but this arrangement meant I'd be seeing Gemma again. Almost every rehearsal, from now until opening night. And nobody else would be in the audience to see us together. Or to distract us. Including my best friends.

"Yes," I blurted. "I'll do it."

I was so happy right then that I almost danced. But I couldn't. Not there in the classroom with Mr. Torres.

So I ate the cookie.

21

"O, what learning is!"
—*Romeo and Juliet*, III.iii.160

At lunch, Tessa was sulking.

"Mr. Torres could've asked *me* to help Liam," she said. "*I'm* the only one of us who went to theater camp. And took a whole workshop on performing Shakespeare!"

"Yes, but Mercutio is a major part," Lucy said. "Mr. Torres knows you don't have the time, Tessa, right?"

Tessa shrugged. "I guess. But Liam knows me. He trusts me."

"And aren't you happy that Mattie's working with him? It's got to help him feel better, don't you think? And it'll be great for the whole play." Lucy's eyes were shining, as if we'd solved the Liam problem.

"Hey, guys, don't expect miracles," I said. "I really don't know what I'm doing, and Romeo's a hard part."

By then, I was starting to get nervous. I didn't even know if Liam knew about the Romeo tutoring, or whatever Mr. Torres wanted us to call it. So it was possible that Liam would feel humiliated about being singled out, taken out of English class, and having to practice with someone who'd only first read the play a few weeks ago and was a complete newbie as an actor. Plus, I'd never even had a one-on-one conversation with Liam before. He was a friend of Willow's, on her (figurative) team, not to mention her crush. She hated me enough to exclude me from her party—and now she hated me even more for crashing it. Probably Liam had to hate me too, out of loyalty to Captain Willow. At the least, he'd resent me for acting all Shakespeare Nerdgirl at him.

But when I arrived at English that afternoon, Mr. Torres said Liam was already waiting for me in the auditorium.

"He's very grateful," Mr. Torres told me quietly. "There won't be any problem, I'm sure of it."

Which made me realize that he'd been worried, too.

I went into the auditorium. Liam was sitting in the front row, staring at his phone. I stood in front of him to let him finish whatever he was looking at.

"Hi, Mattie," he said, looking up at me after a minute. "Looks like you're my rehearsal dummy."

"Excuse me?"

"Nah, that was just a joke. It's really nice of you to help out. Thanks." He smiled at me in a way that was supposed to give me a crush on him, I figured. Like it probably would with all the other girls in our grade.

I couldn't help wondering if he'd tried that smile on Gemma.

"You want to get started?" I said, breaking off eye contact. "I was thinking maybe we'd read the balcony scene."

"Sure. I'll be Juliet, you be Romeo."

"What?"

"Joking again. You don't like jokes, Mattie?"

"I do. I love jokes. I just think we should take this seriously, don't you?" *God, listen to me. I sound so stuck-up. Why am I acting like this?*

Because I'm nervous.

Well, but he's nervous too. So if we're both nervous, how is that helping?

We climbed onstage.

I took three deep breaths. *Relax,* I commanded myself. *Breathe.*

"Okay," I said. "Let's start where Juliet thinks she's talking to herself. She's saying all that stuff about names, how they don't matter. Like if you picked a rose and called it something else—a dandelion, say, or a stinkweed—it would still *smell* like a rose, right? Because the name isn't important."

"But that's not true," Liam said. "Because if you know you're smelling a rose, you *expect* it to smell a certain way. But if you know you're sniffing stinkweed, you're like this." He scrunched up his face and waved his hand in front of his nose.

"Yeah, well," I said, "the point Juliet's making is that Romeo would be the same person if his last name wasn't Montague."

"But how does she know that? If he had a different family maybe he would act completely different."

"True. But can we just—"

"Whatever. Go ahead."

I exhaled. "Okay. So when Juliet realizes someone's been listening to her, she asks what he calls himself, and Romeo says:

> 'By a name
> I know not how to tell thee who I am:
> My name, dear saint, is hateful to myself,
> Because it is an enemy to thee;
> Had I it written, I would tear the word.'

"That means—" I began.

"Nah, I can figure it out," Liam interrupted. "If she

hates his name, he does too. If he'd written his name on a piece of paper, he'd shred it."

"Yes, that's exactly—"

"Dude is messed up," Liam continued. "Because, I mean, it's his *name*. It means *something*, right? And he's like, *I'll do anything for you, Juliet, I'll erase my name. I just met you at this party fifteen minutes ago, but I'll, like, destroy my whole identity for you.*"

"That's true," I admitted. "Romeo does go there really fast."

"He's crazy. All that after kissing her one time?"

"Well, twice."

"Right, twice. And then he's like, *I don't care if your kinsmen, or your guards, or whatever, kill me.* I mean, come on, man. That doesn't even make any *sense*."

"Okay," I said. "I'm not arguing with you, Liam. But that's just how Romeo is."

"Then he's a jerk. He should just be like, *Yeah, I love Juliet, everybody. Deal with it.*"

"But he can't. Or he thinks he can't."

"Why not?" Liam blinked at me from under his long blond hair.

"Because of the feud," I said. "He thinks nobody he knows will understand his feelings."

"So, about that," Liam said. "Maybe he can't talk to

his parents, but he's got these friends, right? Benvolio and Mercutio. Has he talked to *them* about his feelings? He doesn't give them a chance! Maybe he thinks they never loved anyone like how he loves Juliet, but they could still help him decide what to *do*, you know? At least they could listen. But it's like Romeo's in his own head all the time. And that's his problem."

I stared at Liam. What he was saying was really smart. And it was like the gods of theater or Shakespeare's ghost or something like that had sent him here to say those words. To *me*.

"You okay?" he asked.

"Me? No, I'm fine. It's just . . . I agree with you."

Liam nodded. "I mean, Friar Lawrence is *sort* of a friend, but he's too old, and anyway, he's a monk. And Juliet doesn't even *have* any friends. Which is ridiculous."

"You're right."

"I *know* I am." Liam smiled at me again. "Hey, Mattie. Let me know if you need any more help with the play."

We finally did start reading the lines aloud that period, and Liam did fine. His main problem was that he overfocused. He'd start thinking about something Romeo said—one line, one image, one word sometimes—and then he just couldn't get past it. Or he'd decide something Romeo did was stupid, and then he wouldn't shut up about how "no normal guy" (meaning himself) would ever behave like that. Not that he was wrong, for the most part.

Mr. Torres had already figured out Liam's other problem: the way he freaked out whenever people were watching, even other people in the cast. Working with me, though, he didn't purposely ask dumb questions, or waste time the way he did at rehearsals, and he had no trouble reading the lines, or even showing emotion.

But that afternoon, as he rehearsed Romeo's scene with Friar Lawrence (when Romeo tells Friar Lawrence that he wants to marry Juliet that very day), Liam started reciting in that flat, dull way again. I was sitting in the third row of the auditorium, taking notes in the back of my English binder, but compared to Elijah, Liam was so quiet I could barely hear him. A couple of times Mr. Torres told him to "speak up," but it didn't help. Also, Liam kept saying he "didn't understand" why Romeo wanted to get married right away; he'd only met Juliet the night before at the costume party, and now they were eloping?

"That makes no sense, man," Liam kept repeating.

"Yes, and that's what Friar Lawrence is *telling* him," Elijah said.

I could see that Elijah was getting exasperated. He kept trying to catch my eye, the way Gemma did, but I ignored him. I wasn't on Liam's side, exactly, but after he'd said that thing to me about Romeo and his friends, it felt as if we had a connection. Also, I knew he actually cared about the play—but he didn't want other kids, especially boys, to know it.

I saw the look of panic on Liam's face at the end of rehearsal, when Mr. Torres mentioned casually that it might be a "smart idea to start learning lines over the weekend."

"Already?" Liam said. His voice cracked. "I have a ton of hockey practice on Saturday, Mr. Torres. And we have an away game on Sunday in Mantua."

Poor Liam, I thought. I'd had no idea hockey took up so much time.

Mr. Torres shrugged. "Sure. No big deal if this weekend's not convenient, but I'm recommending that the leads begin memorizing. Everyone needs to be completely off-book after winter break. Some people need a little more time to learn lines, so if you've never studied a part before, I'd suggest getting a head start."

"I already started," Elijah said. "Last week."

Show-off. Puke-stocking.

"That's great, Elijah," Mr. Torres said. He smiled at me, but his eyes were darting. *He's nervous. Uh-oh.* "Mattie, you'll help Liam with the memorization, too, right?"

I almost choked on my grape-lemonade Trident. My favorite teacher was obviously losing it. How much did he expect me to do here?

"Oh, sure," I said. "Of course."

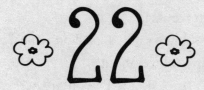

22

"Shall I hear more,
or shall I speak at this?"
—*Romeo and Juliet*, II.ii.39

"I don't believe this," Tessa wailed. "You get to spend every single English class alone with Liam, and now Mr. Torres *also* wants you to help him memorize? You'll be with him so much you guys will be a couple by winter break, I just know it."

I rolled my eyes. "Pass the M&M's, okay?"

That Saturday Lucy and I were over at Tessa's gorging on the Halloween candy rejected by her mom. Tessa had recited her Queen Mab speech at us five times, until even she admitted she had it nailed. So now we were in the pigging-out phase of the afternoon.

"So did Liam smile at you that way he smiles?" Tessa was asking as she chomped on a fun-size Snickers.

I admitted he had.

"And? Aren't I right? Isn't he ridiculously cute?"

"I can see why you'd think so," I said carefully. "I also think he's pretty smart."

"Seriously?" Lucy said. "Based on what?"

"Just stuff we talked about."

"Omigod," Tessa shouted. "You *talked*?"

"Well, sure. We can't rehearse if we don't talk. Listen, Tessa, you don't need to be jealous, I *promise*."

"Yeah? Why not?"

"First of all, *you* like him. Second of all, I may . . . like someone else."

Lucy looked at me with wide eyes.

Tessa didn't see. "Not Elijah, I hope," she said, snorting.

"No. Definitely not Elijah."

"Woo, she's finally decided! So who is it, then? Don't tell me: It's Ajay."

"Are you insane, Tessa?" Lucy squealed.

"Of course I am. So does the Mystery Person know?"

"Absolutely not," I said.

"Hmm. Is it someone I know?"

"Yes."

"Okay, I give up. Who?"

Lucy was nodding slightly, like she was urging me on. Rooting for me, almost. *You can do this*, her eyes told me. *Breathe, Mattie.*

I almost said it then. I did. Because I hadn't stopped thinking about what Liam said about Romeo, how talking to friends might have helped him think straight.

But I just couldn't get the words out. By now I was okay with Lucy knowing, especially because she'd never brought it up again. So I felt I could trust her to keep it to herself. But Tessa? She was just so *loud* about everything. And if she blabbed about it at school, and people heard, who knew what could happen?

I mean, at rehearsal the other day, Willow had scolded Ajay for using the word *gay* as if it was an insult, or something. Most kids I knew would probably say being gay was fine, blah-blah-blah. But knowing that an *actual girl* in middle school had a crush on *another actual girl*? Possibly they wouldn't giggle and tease, but I wouldn't bet on it.

Also, I didn't know how Gemma would react. That could be the worst part.

What if she freaked out and never wanted to talk to me again?

"I'm just not ready," I said. "I can't."

Tessa tore off the wrapping of a KitKat bar with her teeth. "Sure, Mattie," she said. "More secrets, huh?"

Dang. "It's not like that," I said.

"Yeah?" She looked at me with huge, hurt eyes. "What's it like, then?"

"Come on, Tessa," Lucy said. "Mattie will tell us when she's ready. Don't force her."

"I'm not forcing anybody," Tessa said. "I just think if one of your best friends has a crush, she should share the information. I don't keep anything from either of *you*."

It was true; she didn't. She shared everything. And that was the problem.

"I'm really sorry, Tessa," I said.

She shrugged. And if she caught that I'd apologized to her, but not to Lucy, she didn't say.

23

"Tut! I have lost myself; I am not here;
This is not Romeo, he's some other where."
—*Romeo and Juliet*, I.i. 200–201

I felt jittery all Monday morning. Jittery at breakfast, jittery on the walk to school, jittery when Tessa greeted me in homeroom.

"Good morrow, fairest Matilda," she said, bowing. Thereby letting me know she was not still pouting about the crush business. Which was a big relief, obviously—but at the same time, it made me feel guilty. Tessa was a great friend, so *shouldn't* I trust her to keep a secret? How could I be close to someone I *didn't* trust? *Maybe I wasn't being fair to her,* I thought. But if she messed up, it wouldn't be fair to *me*.

At the start of English class, I checked in with Mr. Torres, then went straight to the auditorium. This time Liam was playing something on his phone, so I was okay with interrupting.

"Hey," I said, trying to sound cheerful. "Did you have a nice weekend memorizing lines?"

I meant it as a joke, but by the look on his face I could tell he thought I was serious. And he wasn't happy I'd brought it up.

"No," he muttered. "There are just too many of them. I can't do it, Mattie."

"Sure you can, Liam," I said. "You get this play really well. What you said about Romeo on Friday—I was thinking about it all weekend."

"Yeah?"

I nodded. "Thanks for helping me understand it. Anyway, we'd better get started. You want to go over that scene again with Friar Lawrence?"

"Not really," Liam said, running his fingers through his hair.

"Okay, then what if we practiced for today's rehearsal? It's a fun scene with the Nurse who comes to Romeo with a message from Juliet. All the scenes with the Nurse are so funny, don't you think?"

He shrugged. "Sure, Mattie. If that's what you consider funny."

Why was he being so difficult today? It was like dealing with my little brothers. "Okay, let's start where Mercutio is teasing Romeo about running away from them last night."

I read Mercutio's lines the way I thought Tessa would, except instead of swooshing my arms around, pretend sword-fighting, I did a Darth Vader–y lightsaber sort of move. Whatever it looked like, I have to admit, I *sounded* pretty good. But Liam said his lines as if he were standing on line in the cafeteria, deciding between the hamburger or the hot dog. So it sounded weird when Mercutio tells Romeo that he's glad the old, fun-loving Romeo is back—because the last thing Liam seemed was fun-loving.

"Okay, we'll skip the part when Mercutio is teasing the Nurse," I said, glancing at my watch. "Let's do the conversation between the Nurse and Romeo. The Nurse is annoyed with Mercutio for teasing her, and Romeo tries to calm her by saying Mercutio is a 'gentleman that loves to hear himself talk, and will speak more in a minute than he will stand to in a month.'"

"Mattie, you have that memorized?"

"What?"

"You didn't look at the script when you said Romeo's line just now. It's like you just *knew* it."

"Well, yeah," I said. "It's not so hard to remember."

"Maybe for you." He kicked an imaginary pebble.

"Okay, Liam, is something wrong?" I asked.

"Nah," he said, staring past me, at the stage. "I was

just thinking. When do we put on this play?"

"In about eleven weeks. Which is nine weeks of rehearsal. More or less."

"That's when the ice hockey finals are. If we make it this year."

"Cool," I said. "So Romeo says—"

"And when's the Valentine's Dance?"

"What?"

"The eighth-grade dance. You know."

"A week after the play, I think. You can look all that stuff up online. There's a calendar."

"Yeah, right. So can I ask you a question?"

"Sure. That's why I'm here."

"It's not about the play."

I was starting to sweat a little. "Okay, but we should be rehearsing now, right?"

"I need a time-out. That's allowed, isn't it?"

"Of course. You wanna go to the bathroom, or—"

"Nah. So, Mattie. About the dance—"

"What about it?"

"Do you know if your friend Lucy is going?"

"*Lucy?*" I blinked. "Don't you mean Tessa?"

"No, I mean Lucy. Your smart friend who's a really good dancer. Do you know if she's going to the dance with anyone?"

Dang. This was out of control. Liam refused to rehearse, and now he wanted to break Tessa's heart.

Well, I wouldn't let him.

"Yes," I said firmly. "I'm pretty sure Lucy asked someone already."

"Really? Who?"

"Elijah." It was just the first name that popped into my head, probably because it had occupied brain space for so long.

"That's insane," Liam said, shaking his hair. "I can't believe *anyone* would like Elijah."

"Well, it's really not your business, is it? And he said yes. So can we please get back to—"

"Right, the play." He sighed. "Whatever. You're Mercutio and I'm Romeo."

"Actually, no. Now I'm the Nurse."

"Hey, Mattie. I have an idea. Why don't you be Romeo and I be the Nurse?"

"That's a joke, right? Ha-ha. I got it this time. It's very funny."

But I wasn't laughing, and neither was Liam.

So now I had another secret. *It isn't fair,* I thought.

Although at rehearsal that Monday afternoon, it occurred to me that maybe Liam's crush on Lucy wasn't the most secret-y secret. I mean, just because *I'd* never noticed that he liked Lucy didn't mean nobody *else* was noticing it. Maybe they were; maybe everyone had been noticing but me.

And the funny thing about noticing: Once you finally do start noticing something, you can't stop. Like how if you suddenly look in the mirror and think, *Omigod, my earlobes don't match*, the rest of the day all you see are EARLOBES. EARLOBES EVERYWHERE. It wasn't as if people suddenly grew earlobes overnight, or you'd mistakenly entered Earlobe World—just that you began noticing earlobes.

So maybe that was why as I sat in the third row of the auditorium, taking notes about lines to work on with Liam, I couldn't help noticing the way Romeo looked at Benvolio: shyly, and for slightly too long. Sometimes he even blushed a little too—a sure sign of a crush if there was one. Versus the way Romeo looked at Mercutio: a quick glance, no eye contact, no change in skin tone. Was everybody else seeing all this? Was Lucy? Was Tessa? It was crazy to imagine anyone not noticing what now seemed so obvious to me.

And then I had this thought: If Lucy noticed all that stuff about Gemma and me, maybe she wasn't the only one. Maybe other people noticed it too.

Including (but I had no evidence of this) Gemma.

❀ 24 ❀

"A villain, that fights
by the book of arithmetic!"
—*Romeo and Juliet*, III.i.103

The next day during English, Liam didn't say a word about Lucy or the Valentine's Dance. But he was even more distracted than usual. That afternoon Mr. Torres was rehearsing the scene when the Nurse tells Juliet about Romeo's plan to meet at Friar Lawrence's cell to get married—and since Romeo wasn't in that scene, we had nothing to prepare. So I thought it made sense to go over old stuff—like the *Romeo, Romeo, wherefore art thou Romeo?* scene on the balcony.

But every time I tried to get Liam to focus, he cracked a joke, or texted someone, or had a sudden urge to tie his shoelace. Once, he asked if we could take a break, and I said, "From *what*? We haven't *done* anything yet."

"Aww, come on, Mattie," he said, smiling the Smile. "Don't you get tired of being Mr. Torres's pet?"

"I'm not his pet," I growled.

"Sure you are. That's why you're here, right?"

"I'm here because Mr. Torres asked me. Because he was worried about you."

Liam's eyes narrowed. "He told you that?"

"No," I said immediately, realizing that I'd just said the All-Time Stupidest Thing You Could Say to a Person Freaking About Playing the Lead. "He just wants you to relax. Look, Liam, if you want me to go away—"

"Nah. You should stay."

Although I couldn't figure out what for. He almost seemed as if he didn't care. As if by now he'd decided that being Romeo was impossible, and there was no point even trying.

So then I started to freak, too.

I have to tell Mr. Torres, I thought. My failure as a Romeo tutor had to be obvious to him at every rehearsal, but still, maybe he thought the situation wasn't hopeless. And if he did think that, he needed to hear the truth.

So that afternoon I went to the auditorium, even though technically, without Liam, I shouldn't have been there. I climbed onstage. Mr. Torres was busy talking to Keisha, but right away Gemma came running over.

"Mattie! Where have you been? I haven't seen you in ages!" She gave me a hug that threw me off balance. I almost fell, too, but my backpack strap caught on the arm of a chair that Mr. Torres had placed onstage for the scene.

She couldn't help laughing. "Are you all right?"

"Fine," I said. And even though I'd come on a bad mission, I found myself grinning stupidly. Gemma was looking especially pretty that day, even by Gemma standards: Her cheeks were glowing, and she had on silver earrings that looked like dolphins. Or possibly they were question marks; I didn't get a close look.

"Are you here to watch?" she asked. "Liam's not in the scene today."

"I know," I said, inhaling the powdery Gemma smell.

She smiled. "Are you here to watch *me*, then?"

"What?" I felt my cheeks burn. "*No*. No, I need to— Excuse me."

I scurried over to Mr. Torres, who was still talking to Keisha.

"The Nurse is teasing Juliet here, making her wait for news about Romeo—Mattie? Did you want to speak to me?" He looked surprised.

I nodded. "Can we please talk in private?"

"Of course. Keisha, why don't you start reading with Gemma? I'll be right there. What's going on?"

"Mr. Torres," I said, taking a breath. "I don't think I'm helping Liam."

"Sure you are. He seems more settled. He isn't questioning as much at rehearsal."

"Maybe, but—"

"Try to relax, okay? No one's expecting you to turn him into Benedict Cumberbatch." He raised his eyebrows; I could tell he was wondering if I even knew who that was.

"Mr. Torres, Liam isn't listening to me! He just acts like he doesn't want to be there!"

"You know, Mattie," Mr. Torres said, "sometimes it's hard for certain kids to admit they need help. Especially kids who think of themselves as cool, or who are used to being successful. You get what I'm saying?"

"I *do* get it. But that's not the problem!"

He checked his watch. "Okay, I see we need more time to talk. Can you stop by before homeroom tomorrow?"

I exhaled. "Definitely."

He smiled encouragingly, as if I were the one who was psyched out. "It will be fine, Mattie, I promise. All right, humans, let's begin," he shouted. "Act Two, Scene Five."

Maybe I could have talked to my friends about the Liam situation without spilling the news about his Valentine's Dance question, but I didn't want to risk it. So when Tessa texted me that evening asking, *what's up, saucy wench???* I just responded: *Need to help Mason with homework now. BOOORING. See you tmrw! :)* Usually she didn't stop texting until it got so late she absolutely had no choice but to start on her homework, but luckily, that evening she left me alone.

In the morning, Mom and Dad seemed suspicious about my need for an early ride.

"Mattie, tell us the truth," Dad said as he drank his coffee. "Did you fail another math test? Are you going in early to get extra help?"

"No," I said. "I'm helping one of the actors. But I need to talk to Mr. Torres about it."

Mom frowned. "Mattie, I don't want this play to take over your life."

"It isn't."

"You sure you're passing math this quarter?"

"Yep."

"We could e-mail your math teacher any time," Dad warned.

"Fine with me. Can one of you drive me over to school now?"

"I can," Mom said. "And I can *also* come in with you to say hi to the math teacher."

"I'm not going to Mr. Peltz! Mom, I told you—I'm going to see Mr. Torres!"

I could see the lights flashing in Mom's head: *Mattie's turning into Cara! Here we go again! Fasten your seat belts!*

"Well, maybe I won't drive you *anywhere* if you use that tone with me," she said.

"Never mind." I grabbed a bagel. "I'll walk."

"Don't be silly; it's raining," Mom said, sighing. "I'll drive you. But don't get crumbs in the car."

"And don't be cutting corners on your math homework," Dad called after me, as if we'd been discussing math or homework or corners for the last half hour, and he wanted to leave me with an inspiring thought.

AAARGH, I thought. No wonder Romeo and Juliet couldn't talk to their parents. They were crazy, all of them.

I didn't say anything to Mom the whole car ride, which wasn't as awkward as it sounds, because she had the radio on. But just as we pulled up to school, she asked if I'd had any more thoughts about the Valentine's Dance. I told her I hadn't.

Mom pursed her lips. "You're *not* wearing that Darth Vader costume, you know."

"Mom, I said it was a joke!"

"Well, don't ask me to go dress shopping the weekend before the dance, that's all I'm saying, Mattie."

"I promise I won't. *If* I'm going. And I'm probably not, so . . ." I shrugged. "Thanks for driving."

Mom reached over to brush the bangs out of my eyes. Then she kissed my cheek. "You're welcome, sweetheart. Hurry inside so you don't get wet. And study for math!"

25

"What's in a name? That which we call a rose
By any other name would smell as sweet."
—*Romeo and Juliet*, II.ii. 43–44

As soon as I stepped into Mr. Torres's empty classroom, I could tell something had happened. Something bad.

He looked awful. Not just tired: pale and pinched. He was sitting at his desk, his head in his hands.

"What's going on?" I asked.

"Liam's out of the play," he said.

"*What?*"

"Yep." Mr. Torres took a sip out of his empty-author-head mug. "I just got off the phone with his parents. Apparently, there was a collision on the rink during ice hockey practice early this morning. They're at the ER now. Looks like a broken arm."

"But that's not so bad! Liam can still do the part with a cast on his arm—"

"That's what I told his parents. He's insisting he can't."

I sank into a chair. "He's just making an excuse."

Mr. Torres didn't argue. "I tried to convince him. I even suggested taping his lines to his cast. I know that memorizing was a concern for him."

"Yeah," I said. "One of them. I think he was mostly worried about how he looked to his friends. I'm really sorry."

"No need to apologize, Mattie. You worked hard, and I shouldn't have put you in this position."

"It's okay. I didn't mind. I love working on the play." I took a breath. "Mr. Torres, can I ask you a question? Why *did* you cast Liam as Romeo? I mean, aside from looks."

He smiled a little. "Well, I know he was putting on the dumb-athlete act for his friends, but he's no dummy."

"I agree."

"Plus, he genuinely wanted the part—at first, anyway. And the thing about being a teacher is, you never bet against your students. You always give them a chance to do their best." Mr. Torres got up from his desk, pulled a chair over to me, and sat down. "Speaking of which, Mattie, I want to discuss something."

My stomach flipped over. *What?*

Or maybe I said it aloud: "What?"

He leaned forward. "The question I've been asking

myself is: Can we salvage the production if one of our leads drops out three weeks into rehearsal? I would hate to think the answer is no. Wouldn't you?"

I nodded.

"So what I'm wondering is: Is there someone we can substitute for Liam? Someone who not only has good dramatic skills, but who understands the play, learns fast, and memorizes easily. Someone I can rely on. Someone who's been to almost all of the rehearsals. Know anyone like that?"

I shook my head.

"Come on, Mattie," Mr. Torres said. "It's you, of course."

I kept shaking.

"Why not?" he asked.

I can't play Romeo if Gemma is Juliet. I just can't.

"Mattie?" Mr. Torres said gently. "Can you tell me why not?"

"I'm not an actor," I blurted. "I've only ever been a Narrator. I'm the worst at costumes, I didn't go to theater camp, I can't fence—"

"Neither can anyone else. We'll teach you some moves."

"I can't do love scenes."

"Ditto. They're awkward for everyone. And we'll deal with the kissing stuff—don't worry."

Oh, god. The kissing stuff.

With everyone watching.

Help.

"But what about Paris?" I asked desperately.

"We'll get someone else to play Paris. That won't be a problem; it's a small part. And don't forget, I wanted you to take a bigger part, anyway."

Poor Paris. Always pushed aside by Romeo.

"Listen, Mattie," Mr. Torres said, not letting me look away. "I could hold auditions for Romeo, but we simply don't have time. We're already behind schedule, and we can't afford anything that would set us back further—not to mention the disruptiveness of people swapping parts, or taking on new kids who haven't been rehearsing with us from day one. I know I'm putting you on the spot here, and I know it's completely unfair, so if you're not up to it, just say so, and I won't ask you again."

I couldn't answer; my mouth wouldn't work.

"Of course, if you don't do it, we'll probably have to cancel the production. I know a lot of people will be disappointed—like Tessa, who's *meant* to play Mercutio. And Lucy and Elijah and Keisha and everybody else . . ."

Gemma. Don't forget Gemma.

"Also, if you need more incentive, I guarantee unlimited cookies. Baked for you personally by my wife. Here's a preview." He went to his closet and got a small round container, which he handed to me. "Go ahead, take off the lid."

Not knowing what else to do, I did.

I stared at the cookies.

They were chocolate. Chocolate with chocolate chunks, some of them still gooey.

"Will you at least think about it, Mattie?" Mr. Torres asked in almost a begging voice.

As the chocolate molecules entered my nostrils, filling my head with chocolaty warmth and goodness, I realized that I didn't have a choice. Everything was conspiring against me. Even the cookies.

And I couldn't bear to imagine the look on Gemma's face when she heard the play was being canceled. Because of me. And how she'd think that underneath the Darth Vader costume, I was just a girl talking into a voice thingy. Scared of the spotlight. Scared of everything.

"All right, I'll do it," I said.

"I knew you would," Mr. Torres replied, grinning.

Liam must have texted a bunch of people that morning, because word about his hockey accident spread fast. I listened for my name in the middle of the muttering and cursing and whispering, but it seemed that no one knew yet that Mr. Torres had asked me to play Romeo. Which was a good thing, because I needed Lucy and Tessa to know it first.

I told them at lunch.

"Dude, that's awesome!" Tessa shouted. "*You're* awesome! You're like the picture in the dictionary under the *word* 'awesome'!" Her forehead puckered. "But is Liam hurt badly?"

"Nah, his arm is broken, but he'll be fine," I said.

"You'll be a million times better than him, Mattie," Lucy said. "And it'll be so fun; we can practice together, and everything."

She did a little happy dance in her seat, then bit into her cheese sandwich. I watched her closely. Lucy didn't seem the slightest bit disappointed that she wouldn't be playing Liam's cousin-slash-best-friend. So apparently the Liam–Lucy crush was a one-way thing. Well, that was a relief, considering I'd turned down Liam's invitation for her. One less thing to worry about—and sometime, when Tessa wasn't around, I'd tell Lucy about his crush.

When Tessa got up from the table to get herself a bag of chips, Lucy turned to me. "So are you going to tell her?" she asked quietly.

"You mean Tessa? About what?" I asked.

"Gemma, obviously. You have *other* secrets?"

"No!" I took a bite of my taco to steady myself. Then I said, "Lucy, I *want* to tell her. I just don't know if I *should*."

"Tessa loves you," Lucy said. "She'd do anything for you, Mat."

"Yeah, I know she would. But—"

"And I hate being a part of a secret from her. It feels wrong."

"I know. I'm sorry."

"You don't need to apologize to *me*. That's not why I said it." She sipped her water. "You're not embarrassed, are you?"

"About Gemma? Of course not!"

"So what's the problem, then?"

I took a second. "I'm just scared," I admitted. "What if Tessa says something—not on purpose—and people hear, and are weird about it? What if they start teasing? Or are stupid, or horrible?"

"Mattie," Lucy said warmly. "People respect you; they always have. Just keep acting normal, like you have nothing to hide. Which you don't."

I sighed. "I don't know if I trust people that much, Lucy. Remember when Ajay called Romeo gay?"

"Yes, and no one let him be a jerk! Look, here comes Tessa," Lucy added quickly. "Will you please think about it, Mattie?"

Think about it? No problem. All I ever do is think about it.

26

"If I profane with my unworthiest hand
This holy shrine, the gentle fine is this:
My lips, two blushing pilgrims, ready stand
To smooth that rough touch with a tender kiss."
—*Romeo and Juliet*, I.v.95–98

In English class later that afternoon, Mr. Torres made the announcement: "Of course, we're all disappointed that Liam can't continue as Romeo, but we're so lucky that Mattie has agreed to step into the role."

The class went silent.

Then Willow exploded. "*What?* Seriously, Mr. Torres, *Mattie*?"

"What's the problem?"

"It'll *look* wrong! It'll be distracting. Isn't there a *boy*—"

"Willow, Tybalt's a boy," Tessa said. "Should we get a boy to play Tybalt instead of *you*?"

"Romeo's different," Willow insisted. "He's the love interest."

"And Mattie will have to kiss Gemma," Charlotte said.

"So what?" Tessa argued. "You know, in Shakespeare's production, two boys played Romeo and Juliet, so *they* had to kiss, right? And *Shakespeare* didn't get distracted. He was fine with it!"

"This is true," Mr. Torres said. "And the important thing is that Mattie is an excellent actor who deserves our support. It's very brave of her to step into a challenging role a few weeks into rehearsal. Basically, it's thanks to her that we still *have* an eighth-grade production this year."

Nobody clapped or anything.

"Mr. Torres, what if *I* try talking to Liam?" Willow said. "He listens to me."

Tessa made a face at me from across the room.

"You can if you want, Willow, but I don't know how much good it'll do. It sounds like he's made up his mind," Mr. Torres said.

"I'll go to his house right after school today," Willow announced. "Maybe if someone talks to him in person, it'll help."

Then she looked at me with narrowed eyes, as if someone had stolen something from Liam, or from her, or from both of them, or from *everybody*, and I was the prime suspect.

While Willow was off persuading Liam to rejoin the play, Mr. Torres canceled regular rehearsal that afternoon and met with Gemma and me in his classroom.

"We're going to need to take it up a notch after Thanksgiving," he said. "Can you guys come to school early in the mornings for some extra practice?"

Gemma winced. "I'll try. I'm not a morning person, really."

"Neither am I," Mr. Torres admitted. "But we'll need to retrace our steps for a bit."

"How long is 'a bit'?" I asked nervously.

"That's really up to you, Mattie," Mr. Torres answered. "However long it takes for you to feel comfortable with the role. Of course, the sooner the better, but I'm not using a stopwatch. All right, shall we tackle the costume party scene, omitting for now all the kissing stuff?"

Gemma did her rowdy laugh. "Oh yes, for Mattie's sake. I had a tuna sandwich for lunch, and it had onions."

I don't remember much from that first rehearsal with Gemma. The whole thing was so strange—being inside a scene that I'd only ever read, or watched, from the outside. And at the same time, feeling like I was also in a parallel universe, listening to myself saying loving words to Gemma. Not *my* words, obviously, and not my exact emotions, but Shakespeare's beautiful words of love ("Did my heart love till now? Forswear it, sight!

192 ☼ BARBARA DEE

For I ne'er saw true beauty till this night"). And hearing Gemma say beautiful words back at me—without meaning anything by them. Without knowing that *I* meant anything either.

Although there was one moment during that rehearsal that I kept thinking about the whole walk home, and at dinner, and all evening, and then all Thanksgiving weekend: when we touched hands. Gemma's hands were soft and warm, and mine were cold and damp with nerves, but when we touched she looked right at me. Into my eyes. And she didn't make a joke about my hand temperature or cringe or tell me to put on gloves. She just said, "Oh."

I couldn't stop wondering what it meant, that "oh." Maybe it was an "oh" of shock, like: *Yeow, your hands are super freezing! Were you frozen in carbonite, Mattie?* Or maybe it was something else. An "oh" of understanding. Like: *Oh yes, now I get it.*

But that was silly. How much information could you get just from touching someone's hand? *Not much,* I told myself. *Don't overanalyze, Mattie.*

Anyhow, it was a long rehearsal. Mr. Torres seemed happy with how it went, although I had the feeling that he mostly wanted to act positive and encouraging. He told us to meet him on Monday morning at seven fifteen, gave us both high fives, then left the room.

"Good rehearsal," Gemma said as we were putting on our jackets.

"You too," I replied automatically.

"You're a bit nervous, yeah?"

"A bit."

Gemma smiled sweetly. "Don't be. You'll be an amazing Romeo, I can tell."

She gave me a quick, powder-scented hug and ran off.

Oh, I kept thinking. *Oh*.

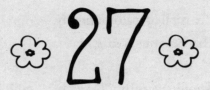

27

"Thy head is as full of quarrels
as an egg is full of meat."
—*Romeo and Juliet*, III.i.23–24

The following Monday morning, Gemma and I did the costume party scene again, still putting off what Mr. Torres called "the kissing stuff." I couldn't tell if he liked my acting or if he just didn't want to scare me off, but when kids started showing up for homeroom, he flashed a grin, told me I'd done great, and that he'd see me in English. For a second I stood there, confused. But then I remembered that if Liam was out of the play, that meant I was back in class. Which I was happy about, truthfully. I missed going to my favorite subject.

Although that afternoon, just before Mr. Torres showed up in his classroom, Willow reported that she had bad news. "Liam says he won't do the play. He'll be back in school tomorrow, and he doesn't want anybody pressuring him, okay?"

"No one would," Ajay said. "He's a sucky Romeo, anyway."

"Did Liam say *why* he was dropping out?" Elijah asked. "Because it can't just be about his arm."

"I agree," Willow said. "I think he got psyched out somehow." She did a funny thing then. She looked at *me*. As if *I* were the reason Liam was psyched out.

"You know," I said, my heart pounding, "I was trying to *help* him, Willow."

"Yeah, Mattie. Great job."

"Seriously, Willow?" Tessa said. "You're implying that Mattie—"

"Hey, I'm not implying anything. I'm just saying *great job helping Liam.* You know, because his confidence was really getting *boosted.*" She rolled her eyes.

"Liam's confidence doesn't need boosting," Elijah said. "He has nothing *but* confidence. No brains."

"Wait, that isn't fair," I said.

Elijah looked at me in surprise. "You're sticking up for him?"

"No. I mean yes. Look, you guys, he tried. It's just a really hard part."

"Not too hard for *you*, though, Mattie," Willow said. "You'll be an awesome Romeo, I'm *sure*."

"Willow, do you have a problem?" Tessa asked loudly.

196 @ BARBARA DEE

"Is there some reason you're against Mattie playing Romeo? Because I'm curious to hear it."

My heart banged. Tessa refused to stop sticking up for me. She was a better friend than I was, really.

"There's no reason," Willow muttered. "I just don't like how this whole thing happened, okay? Where was Mr. Torres? Why didn't he help Liam himself, instead of making Mattie do it for him?"

"Mr. Torres didn't make me," I said. "And he *did* try to help Liam. Then he asked me."

"Yeah, because you're this Shakespeare Nerdgirl, right?" Willow folded her arms across her chest. "Also I'm upset about Liam just giving up."

"Well, don't be," Tessa snapped. "Because he's happy now. He wanted to get out of the play, and he did. Right?"

Willow narrowed her eyes and shrugged.

I could see how much she hated to admit defeat. So maybe that's why she was so mad—she'd ordered Liam to play Romeo again, and he'd refused. It was like a Team Willow mutiny, led by her crush. And the worse part? Her crush would be replaced by *me*, the Evil Party Crasher. Shakespeare Nerdgirl under a Darth Vader helmet.

Who knew the truth about Liam's crush on Lucy. Although Willow didn't know about it. And she didn't know that I knew it.

I figured this gave me a sort of power. Which I'd probably never use, but still.

That afternoon, Romeo and Juliet got married. It's a weird scene, because you don't even get to see the wedding ceremony; it's just Romeo and Friar Lawrence waiting for Juliet to show up. When she does, Friar Lawrence basically tells them: *Okay, you two, since you're so eager to get married, let's get this over with.* The wedding takes place offstage, so the scene has no "kissing stuff," no hand touching, barely any words. The scene is so short that Mr. Torres said he wanted to "push on," blocking the next scene, which was long and full of action.

It was also a scene I'd been dreading. Act Three, Scene One was when Tybalt kills Mercutio (thanks to Romeo's stepping into the middle of their sword fight), and Romeo kills Tybalt in revenge. Love scenes with Gemma were hard; this scene would be hard in a completely different way, and the truth was, I didn't feel ready.

Maybe Gemma realized it. Just before she jumped off the stage to take a seat in the front row, she whispered in my ear, "Hey, Romeo. Don't let Tybalt push you around."

I looked at her in surprise. Did she mean *Willow* shouldn't push *me* around—or was she talking about the play? It was hard to tell.

But I smiled, bowed, and doffed a pretend hat. "A million thanks, sweetest lady."

When I stood, I saw Willow watching us. I turned my head away quickly, so that if I started blushing, she wouldn't see.

"Hey, Mattie," Tessa shouted from across the stage. "You need something to use as a sword. I'm using a pen."

"No pens," Mr. Torres announced. "And no pencils, either, humans. Nothing with a point."

"Oh, come on, Mr. Torres," Willow said. "We're not *really* going to hurt each other."

Mr. Torres took a drink out of a water bottle. "The way this play is going, let's not tempt fate, okay? If you must have a prop, use something with a blunt edge only."

"Like Elijah's head," Ajay suggested.

"Aw, shut up, Ajay, you rat-catcher," Tessa said. I knew she was ecstatic that in this scene, Mercutio gets to call Tybalt "rat-catcher." I didn't know what it meant, exactly (Was it bad to catch rats?), but it was still a great insult. In fact, it almost made up for the fact that Tybalt was about to kill Mercutio.

"Psst, Mattie." Gemma was at the lip of the stage, motioning me over. When I got there, she handed me a straw still in its paper. "Use this," she said. "Remember our sword fight?"

Now I did blush. Of course I remembered: straw versus lightsaber. How she'd vanquished Darth Vader.

"Thank you," I said.

Gemma beamed at me.

"Gems, you have any more of those?" Willow asked.

"Not on me," Gemma replied. "But I got it in the cafeteria at lunch. Shall I go steal some more?"

"Not a bad idea," Mr. Torres said. "All right, then, Benvolio and Mercutio, you're entering the town square. Benvolio is worried that Mercutio is itching for a fight with the Capulets, especially with Tybalt. Let's do this, humans."

Lucy and Tessa walked out onstage together. Tessa was swinging her arms in a looking-for-danger sort of way, but when Lucy begged her to go home instead of looking for a "brawl," Tessa said: "Thy head is as full of quarrels as an egg is full of meat." It was such a great line that Tessa started to laugh.

"This isn't a funny scene, Tessa," Charlotte informed her. "People are about to get killed, you know."

"*I'm* about to get killed, you 'foul undigested lump,' but it's still hilarious."

"Tessa," Mr. Torres warned. "Watch the mouth, please."

"Sorry." She zipped her lip.

"Okay, now Tybalt enters. If Mercutio is itching for a

fight, Tybalt has the chicken pox. Especially for Romeo, who crashed his uncle's party."

"Yeah," Tessa said. "And Tybalt tries to make himself sound all macho and official when he accuses Mercutio of 'consorting' with Romeo. So then Mercutio makes fun of him for using the word 'consort.' Because it's obvious that Tybalt's a jerk."

"It *is*?" Willow growled. "How is Tybalt a jerk?"

"Oh, come on. The way he struts around like he's so great, like he's in charge of everybody, but he isn't. That's why Mercutio calls him 'king of cats.' And then 'rat-catcher.'"

"*And* why Tybalt is sick of all of Mercutio's talking. Because Mercutio never shuts up!"

"Willow, 'were I like thee, I'd throw away myself,'" Tessa quoted.

I burst out laughing; I couldn't help it.

"*Timon of Athens*," Tessa informed me.

"Hey, you guys," Lucy said loudly. "Can we please get back to *this* play?"

"Thank you, Lucy," Mr. Torres said. He was starting to look tired and sweaty, I thought.

Just then Gemma burst into the auditorium waving a fistful of straws. "Success!" she shouted, passing out straws to everyone, even Charlotte, who was Lady Capulet.

And then, of course, everyone started straw-fighting

everybody else, running and chasing each other all over the stage, and up and down the aisles of the auditorium.

It was hilarious.

Once, I poked Gemma in the shoulder. Once, Tessa poked me, calling me a "herd of boils and plagues." So I called her "scurvy knave" and plastic-strawed her in the butt.

We went on like this for about fifteen minutes.

Mr. Torres let us, because truthfully, he had no choice.

28

"It was the lark, the herald of the morn;
No nightingale."
—*Romeo and Juliet*, III.v.6–7

The next day, Liam came back to school with his arm in a cast. I don't know if he expected banners with LIAM, WE BESEECH THEE, PLEASE BE ROMEO AGAIN written in glitter glue. Or possibly he expected people to yell at him. But from what I could see, nobody even mentioned anything about bailing on the play. And by the end of that Friday, Liam was walking around doing the Smile fulltime. I was even glad for him, actually. He wasn't a bad person; he just wasn't tough enough for Shakespeare.

The pre-homeroom rehearsals with Gemma and Mr. Torres went on for a couple more weeks. I guess because it was too early in the morning to fool around, these sessions were pretty much all business. We'd started using the stage in the auditorium, so Mr. Torres could work with me on blocking.

And even though there was barely any time to chat with Gemma, I loved meeting with her to practice our parts in semi-private. She was so smart about everything. If I had trouble pronouncing a word, or knowing where to take a breath, she'd make a suggestion that always helped. If I got tangled up in one of Romeo's speeches, she'd say it to me—not to correct me, but to show how easy it was to understand. If Romeo said something funny, she laughed. If he was being mopey or ecstatic or angry or passionate, I saw it reflected on her face. And that made me believe I could communicate emotions—that if I felt something that Romeo felt, I could make someone else feel it too.

But every morning Gemma was arriving a few minutes later, and I remembered how she'd said that she wasn't a morning person, and how hard it was for her to be on time. Plus, it was mid-December, and the weather was getting worse. I didn't want to force her to keep waking up early, in the icy darkness, coming to school just to help me practice.

One morning a few days before winter break, Gemma was ten minutes later than usual. As we were waiting for her, I told Mr. Torres that I was getting pretty comfortable with playing Romeo, and didn't think we still needed these extra early rehearsals.

"Your call, Mattie," he said. "I'm glad you're feeling

more confident." He studied my face for a few long seconds. "So here's a question for you, then. Does this mean Romeo is ready to deal with the kissing stuff?"

"What?" I didn't see the logic: Dropping early rehearsals meant kissing Gemma Braithwaite? Onstage? In front of people? "You mean *now*?"

"We can wait a bit," he said. "If you need a little more time, no problem. But I think that the longer we put it off, the more awkward it'll be for both of you. Will you give it some thought over winter break?"

I nodded. *Some thought.* Yeah, I could give it plenty of that.

"And how's it going with the memorizing?"

Just fine, I told him. Memorizing was not an issue for me. In fact, it was one of the best things about being in the play: branding Shakespeare's words on my brain forever. I'd even started memorizing some of Juliet's lines, although not on purpose.

Just then Gemma ran into the auditorium. "Sorry I'm late," she said breathlessly, pulling off her blue wool scarf and mittens. "Call from Mummy. She doesn't believe in time zones."

"That's okay," Mr. Torres said, glancing at me. "Mattie was just saying she's ready to end these morning rehearsals, anyway."

Gemma looked startled. "Oh," she said. "Really?"

I nodded. "Yeah, I think I'm doing okay now. As Romeo, I mean."

"All right, then," she said.

She didn't smile. She didn't even look relieved. And I couldn't tell what she was thinking. Maybe it was: *Mattie, I can't believe you think you don't need extra rehearsal time. Because truthfully, you're still a hopeless Romeo.*

Although I doubted that. She'd been so encouraging lately, and so had Mr. Torres. I mean, even *I* could hear how much better I'd been sounding.

But how come she didn't seem happy? I'd canceled rehearsals for her sake, really.

At lunch, Tessa was retaking a math quiz, so I just told Lucy about Gemma's funny reaction.

"Maybe Gemma liked the extra rehearsals," Lucy said, smiling. "And maybe she liked them because she likes *you*."

"Meaning what?" I muttered, checking around our table to make sure no one was eavesdropping.

"Meaning maybe she likes you *back*."

"I really don't think so."

"How do you know that, Mattie? Did you ask her?"

"What? Of course not."

"You could, you know." Lucy carefully peeled a banana.

"Remember how crazy you made yourself over Elijah? Wouldn't it be better to know where you stand with Gemma?"

I couldn't believe this. Lucy had never even had a boyfriend, and here she was, giving me advice about a girlfriend. What could she possibly know about this subject, anyway?

And what if I *did* ask Gemma? Chances were good that she'd answer something like, *Actually, um, I don't like you BACK, I just like you as a FRIEND*—which would turn everything all awkward and sticky between us. Exactly at the moment when I needed to deal with—or get ready to deal with—the onstage-kissing stuff.

And if she gave me the *Actually, um* answer, what would I have to look forward to every day? I wouldn't stop liking her even if she said that; I'd be like Romeo moping for Rosaline. Back to how it felt when I thought I liked Elijah—except knowing that Gemma was the opposite of dirtbag.

Plus, what if Gemma told someone about my question— someone like Willow? I could say, *Here's a question for you, Gemma, but you have to promise to keep it just between us.* Although what would stop Gemma from blabbing even if she promised?

And, okay, maybe she wouldn't talk about it, maybe

she *would* keep a promise—but what if she started acting weird and awkward around me once she gave the *Actually, um* answer? People with crush detectors might figure out what was going on, the way Lucy had. Then play rehearsals would become absolute torture, with everyone staring and giggling whenever we had a love scene, which was ALL THE TIME.

BECAUSE I WAS ROMEO, AND SHE WAS JULIET. So, I mean, *of course* I couldn't ask that question.

Lucy was my best friend, but obviously, she couldn't understand.

29

"I'll send a friar with speed
To Mantua, with my letters."
—*Romeo and Juliet*, IV.i.123–124

Winter break meant two weeks of nonstop relatives—
aunts, uncles, assorted cousins, two sets of grandparents,
three dogs, plus Cara and two of her college friends. Tessa
spent the break with her dad, although she texted me so
often it hardly felt like she was away. I hung out with Lucy
a bunch of times to rehearse our scenes together, and once
we went to the mall with Keisha and Ellie Yamaguchi.

"So are you guys going to Willow's for New Year's Eve?"
Ellie asked as we stood on line for pretzels.

Lucy and I exchanged glances. New Year's Eve was the
very next day, and I hadn't gotten an invitation from Willow. Not that this surprised me.

"Nah, we have something else planned," Lucy said.

"Oh, yeah? What?" Keisha asked.

"Can't say. It's top secret." Lucy nudged me in the ribs, so I nodded.

After the mall, when the two of us were crocheting tiny animals in Lucy's bedroom, I asked Lucy if Willow had invited her.

"Yes, but what difference does it make?" she said. "I'd never go, the way she's been treating Tessa lately. *And* the way she keeps excluding *you*."

"Thank you," I said. It wasn't the first time that I'd thought how Lucy always had my back. "So what's our top secret plan for tomorrow night?"

I said this grinning, sure there wasn't any plan at all.

But Lucy closed her bedroom door. In a quiet voice she said, "I happen to know that Gemma and her dad are back in England for Christmas. So if you wanted to communicate, now would be the perfect time to leave something in her mailbox, or slip it under her door."

"Communicate?" I put down my crochet needle and stared at her. "You mean telling Gemma how I feel? Asking if she feels the same way? Lucy, I already told you—"

"I just mean expressing yourself. You don't even have to sign your name. Then afterward you and I could have a sleepover."

"But what's the point? I mean, if I don't sign my name, she won't know it's from me!"

"Right," Lucy said, as she admired her tiny crocheted chick. "But that's not what matters. I just think you need to get your feelings out somehow, or you'll go crazy. Frankly, I think you're already going crazy."

"You do? Why?"

"Mattie, you're sitting on my bed pulling threads out of my blanket."

"And that equals crazy?"

"You've also been staring off into space."

"Lucy, I always stare off into space."

"True. But when you did it over Elijah, you weren't *also* destroying my blanket."

I left Lucy's house in a sort of stupor. Lucy was my Sensible Friend, the one Mom liked, the one who thought in PowerPoint presentations, everything all logical and numerical. And here she was advising me to do something that *made no sense.*

Except deep down, I knew it did. I *did* need to get my Gemma feelings out. Between wondering how she felt about me and feeling guilty about not telling Tessa, I was barely sleeping most nights this vacation. And with the Kissing Stuff about to happen in three more days, I needed to be well rested and not all eye-baggy.

Plus, as hard as I tried, I couldn't think of a downside to Lucy's plan. Gemma wasn't home, so I didn't have to worry she'd see us creeping around her building. If I didn't sign my name, she'd never know who'd sent the note. I wouldn't even have to disguise my handwriting—I could just type the thing on my computer.

So there weren't even any risks, at least none I could see. Not like there were in asking the Question and getting an *Actually, um* response in return.

Besides, part of me felt mad that I needed to hide my feelings at all. Why should I have to? Everyone else I knew was allowed to have a crush. Even a stupid one.

All right, I'll do it, I told myself. *I'll make a decision, and take action!*

But what to say? The words needed to be perfect.

I went to bed that night still trying to come up with something, and woke up the next morning with an empty head. All day I chatted with cousins and uncles and walked their dogs, telling myself, *Come on, Mattie. Here's your chance to tell Gemma something. What should she know?*

That your mind's a complete and utter BLANK?

Fifteen minutes before I was supposed to meet Lucy, and still desperate for a message, I found myself flipping through *Romeo and Juliet*.

And there they were. The perfect words that captured exactly how I felt:

Heaven is here,
Where Juliet lives; and every cat and dog,
And little mouse, every unworthy thing,
Live here in heaven and may look on her;
But Romeo may not.

But was this speech too much? Did it give too much away?

Stop overthinking, I scolded myself. *It's what you feel, right? So just SAY it, for once.*

I typed it, printed it, and sealed the paper in a plain white envelope.

I didn't tell Lucy what I'd written, and she didn't ask. And before I could stop myself, we slipped the envelope under Gemma's door.

The last day of vacation, Cara put her arm around me.

"French toast?" she asked, raising her eyebrows as if we had a conspiracy.

"You mean now?" I asked. It was four in the afternoon, but she'd just woken up at two, so her time zone was off. Like Gemma's mom, I thought, who didn't believe in them.

"*Absolutely* now," Cara replied. "There's nothing to eat around here, anyway." She grabbed a few Christmas cookies from the kitchen counter and led me to her car.

We drove to Patsy's Diner blaring her car stereo. As soon as we got there and placed our orders, Cara leaned across the sticky table and grabbed my hands. "So, little sister," she said, "what's been going on with you? How's Paris?"

"You mean the city?" I said.

"I mean the character. In your play."

"Oh, *Paris*." It felt like years ago that I was Paris. Although the funny thing was I'd only played him in one rehearsal, and that was only for one line.

"Actually, that's changed," I said. "Mom didn't tell you?"

"Mom never tells me *anything* about you. I think she's afraid I'll control you from afar." She wiggled her fingers at me in a mad-scientist sort of way.

I decided to ignore that. "My teacher switched me. I'm Romeo now."

"Seriously? Are you kidding?"

"Nope."

"Omigod, that's incredible! Congratulations, you little rock star!"

"Stop calling me 'little.'"

"Sorry. You *big* rock star. Wow. So . . . how does it feel?"

I thought about it. "Pretty good, actually. I was really scared at first. But I've had extra rehearsals in the mornings. And now I feel okay about it. But . . ."

"Ah. A 'but.'"

"I have to kiss Juliet starting tomorrow."

"I see. And that's awkward?"

I nodded.

"Well, it's probably awkward for her, too," Cara said.

"Yeah. Except in a different way, maybe."

"What do you mean?"

My heart was racing. Should I tell her? Suddenly, I needed to know my big sister's reaction. "I don't think she cares, actually. Not like I do."

I waited for Cara to nod, or act surprised, or at least ask a follow-up question. But she didn't. She just sat there pouring sugar into her coffee, then adding half-and-half, as if I'd said something perfectly obvious about the weather. Had she even heard what I'd just said? Did she get it? Should I repeat it? Maybe she thought I was too young to mean anything. And really, I hadn't been all that specific, had I?

"All right, so you like this girl," she said matter-of-factly, as if I'd just told her that I had a pebble in my shoe. "And you don't know if she likes you back?"

I ran my finger over some spilled sugar. "She likes me as a friend; I'm sure about that. But that's *all* I'm sure about."

Okay. She *had* to get it now.

I waited, my heart thumping.

Cara sipped her coffee. "Let me ask you something, Mattie. Have you ever kissed a boy?"

"No."

"Too bad. Because kissing a girl works the same way. There's a word for that. Bisexual."

Our French toast arrived. Cara took an enormous bite drippy with syrup. "So," she said. "Tell me about Juliet. The girl playing her."

"Her name is Gemma. She's English. Really smart. And really beautiful."

"Huh." Cara thought it over as she chewed. "She's probably kissed someone before, is my bet."

"Where'd you get that from?"

"Vibes. They never fail me. So my big-sisterly advice to you is: Follow her lead."

"Okay," I said. "Thanks."

I had no idea what that even meant. But now I desperately needed to talk about anything but kissing Gemma, so I asked Cara if she wanted to complain about Mom instead.

30

"Hence from Verona art thou banished:
Be patient, for the world is broad and wide."
—*Romeo and Juliet*, III.iii.15–16

Sunday night, before school started, sleeping was hopeless. I just kept picturing Gemma's dad handing her the envelope. Or Gemma discovering it when she walked in the door. And then bending down, picking it up, opening it. And reading it.

What have I done?

I've made a terrible, no-backsies mistake.

I am a moron.

Why did I let Lucy talk me into it?

And why did I choose that passage? It was as good as signing my name. At least, if I had signed my name, I could feel as if I wasn't holding back. Getting it all out there, whatever happens next.

But using that passage and not signing my name was

just stupid. It was like a love note from Romeo but not Mattie. Which makes me look immature and unbrave.

Of course Gemma wouldn't like me back! Why should she? I'm as reckless as Romeo, but also a total wimp. A reckless wimp: How oxymoronic.

Not knowing what else to do, I got out of bed and practiced Romeo's lines until the sun came up.

On Monday, Mr. Torres was buzzing with energy, like he'd eaten too many of his wife's cookies over winter break.

"Welcome back, humans," he said at the start of English class. "I hope you've all had a restful break, except for the time you've spent memorizing lines."

The class groaned.

He ignored it. "Starting today, we are in phase two of rehearsals, which will last for the next three weeks. I expect all actors to be off-book. That means I don't want to see any scripts in any hands onstage. Your lines should now reside up here." He pointed to his head.

"That should be easy for you, Ajay," Tessa said. "Considering the amount of spare room in your cranium."

"I'll pretend I didn't hear that," Mr. Torres said, not smiling. "Miss Bluestone will be attending rehearsals from now on to cue actors if they miss a line—but you should not use her as your crutch. If you don't have your lines down, get busy! Study your lines at breakfast, while you're brushing your teeth, while you're walking your dog! You'll see on the new schedules I'm handing out that we'll be picking up the pace. Unless a scene is unusually long or complicated, we'll be rehearsing two or three scenes every afternoon. Many of you will also be practicing dance steps and sword-fight moves with our wonderful gym teacher, Ms. Selden. Tech crew people: you'll be working every afternoon in the gym with Mrs. Dimona until we reach phase three."

"What's phase three?" Keisha asked, looking worried.

"Our final two weeks of rehearsal. That's when we put up the set and the lights, fine-tune all scenes, fit the costumes, have our dress rehearsal. Short of an emergency of nuclear proportions, no one will be allowed to miss a single second of phase three."

Liam raised the arm that wasn't in a cast. "What about me?" he asked.

Everyone looked at him.

Mr. Torres sipped some water out of his empty-author-head mug. He didn't seem to be in any hurry to swallow it. "You'll be running props with Miss Bluestone," he said.

I glanced at Tessa. Mr. Torres was not just a great teacher, he was a nice person—but "running props with Miss Bluestone" sounded like a punishment, like Liam was being banished from the play. And it seemed Liam agreed, the way he slumped in his seat. But, of course, he had no right to protest, and everyone knew it.

We spent the rest of that period talking about Romeo's banishment in Act Three. Ajay said he thought it was a pretty lenient sentence, considering that Romeo had killed Tybalt on purpose. Charlotte said she couldn't figure out why Juliet didn't just run off with Romeo. Keisha reminded her that Juliet was still only thirteen. And Willow couldn't stop talking about how horribly Lord Capulet behaved, insisting that Juliet marry Paris immediately, or "hang, beg, starve, die in the streets."

It was an interesting discussion, but I couldn't stay with it. I was thinking about the new rehearsal schedule, specifically the next time I'd be with Gemma. Juliet wasn't due up until tomorrow, so probably I wouldn't see her at all until then. Which meant I wouldn't know if she'd read my note or had figured out who'd sent it. Not that I had any doubts. But if I could just look into her eyes—

"Mattie?" Mr. Torres was standing in front of me with a questioning expression. "Will you begin reading for us?"

I swallowed. "I'm sorry. Starting where?"

Now he frowned at me. "You're not with us today, are you? Please pay attention; we need everyone's complete focus going forward. Willow, will you read for us, please?"

I could feel a slow blush creeping up my neck. As much as I hated being called "teacher's pet," Mr. Torres's approval meant a lot to me. He'd never scolded me before, not even when I'd been giggling with Gemma at rehearsal.

"Ooh, teacher's pet's in time-out," Charlotte whispered. "Naughty, naughty."

"Shut up, Charlotte," I muttered.

You okay? Tessa was mouthing at me from across the room.

I shrugged and stared blindly at my book.

At rehearsal that afternoon, we were back to Act One, Scene One—which was a good thing, because it gave me a chance to act with Lucy. Everything about her was sane and reassuring; she always made me feel as if things were under control.

But as we did our scene as Romeo and Benvolio, I couldn't help noticing that Lucy seemed a little off. I knew from practicing with her over vacation that she had her lines perfectly memorized, but that first off-book rehearsal, she needed several prompts from Miss Bluestone.

"Everything all right?" I asked her when we'd finished for the day.

"Yeah, I guess," she said. "Wanna go get some fro-yo?"

I didn't. Fro-yo in January seemed like a terrible idea,

truthfully. But I could tell Lucy had something on her mind, because she was twisting her hair and not talking. So I agreed.

At Verona's I got a small cup of caramel with hot fudge sauce, and Lucy got a cup of mango with blackberries. By the way she poked at it with her spoon, I could see she wasn't in the mood for fro-yo any more than I was.

"What's up?" I asked. "Something's bothering you, I can tell."

"Yeah," she admitted. "But I'm afraid you'll be mad at me."

"Why would I be?"

"Because I did something crazy today."

"*You?*" I didn't mean to make it sound like *Perfect Lucy made a mistake? Heavens!* But that's what it came out like. "Sorry. What happened?"

She started shredding her napkin. "Somehow Liam got the idea that I'd asked Elijah to the Valentine's Dance. And he said something to Elijah about it—you know, to tease him."

I almost choked on my fro-yo. "How do you know that?"

"Because Elijah told me."

"Huh. Really. And what did you say?"

"Well, Elijah looked confused. You know that thing he

222 @ BARBARA DEE

does with his eyebrows?" Lucy imitated Elijah's confused-eyebrow expression. "And I felt bad for him. He seemed humiliated—I didn't know what else to do!"

"So you asked Elijah to the dance?"

"I don't know even know how it happened; it just came out of my mouth!" Lucy wailed. "But I'll un-ask him if you want."

"Why would I?"

"Oh, Mattie, because he was your crush for an entire year! And Tessa and I said all those horrible things about him—"

"Wait," I said. "Tessa was the one who called him a dirtbag, not you. And anyway, I don't care about him anymore. I promise."

"Well, I wasn't sure if you . . . ," Lucy said. She stopped.

"If I still liked boys?"

She nodded.

"Yeah, I think I do. Just because I'm over Elijah doesn't mean I can't crush on a boy." I took a breath and blurted: "I think I might have blown it with Gemma."

"Why? How?"

I told her which speech I'd put in the envelope, how it had to be obvious who'd sent it.

Lucy didn't argue. She was too good a friend to make up some lame, supportive lie about how Gemma wouldn't assume Romeo = Mattie. "But so what if Gemma knows it was you? That's not the worst thing, right?"

I winced. "Maybe it is. I don't know!"

"Well, try not to worry about what you don't know." She paused. "So you're okay with me going with Elijah? To the dance?"

"Yes," I said firmly. "Yes, I *am* sure about *that*."

Lucy exhaled. "Phew. But please don't tell Tessa about Elijah and me yet. She'll freak when she hears."

I nodded.

Just another item on the list of Secrets We're Keeping from Tessa.

31

You know that feeling when you're on an elevator, and your stomach arrives at the floor an entire second after you do? That's how I felt at school all Tuesday, thinking about seeing Gemma at rehearsal.

But when I got there, everything was fine between us. Weirdly fine. Gemma gave me a Happy New Year hug and asked if I'd had a good winter break. She complained about how much memorizing she'd had to do. She asked if I'd seen a movie I hadn't; we talked about it as if I had. I looked straight into her eyes; she looked right back at me. And that was it.

So I even started not-dreading Thursday, which was when we'd do the costume ball scene again—this time without scripts. But with kissing.

I mean, I was still paralyzed with nerves. But if Gemma hadn't realized I'd written that note—or if, by some miracle, she hadn't read it, possibly because her dad had tossed it, assuming it was junk mail or something—then the kissing might not be unbearable. Might even be *nice*, potentially. If I could do what Cara suggested: Just follow Gemma's lead.

So I wasn't even freaking extra hard when I got to the auditorium Thursday afternoon and saw that she was already onstage, waiting.

As soon as she saw me, she turned her back to put something on her face. It was a pair of red plastic glasses with goo-goo eyes, the kind that bounce around on springs.

"O Romeo, Romeo, wherefore art thou Romeo?" she said in a squeaky falsetto.

I giggled. "Wrong speech. Today we meet at the costume ball and do the hand thing."

"Oh, bollocks. Well, I suppose this will do for my costume, then. Wouldn't you fall in love with me dressed like this?"

I didn't answer.

"Let me see *you* in these, Mattie." Gemma took off the goo-goo glasses and put them on my face.

I breathed in her Gemma smell as she straightened the frames at my temples.

"Ooh yes, thunderbolts! I'd be smitten with you instantly." She giggled. "You're so much googly-er than that horrible Liam. Do you know what that dimwit did?"

"No," I said.

"When I was back in the UK during Christmas, he came round my flat, apparently, and put a love-poem-y thing under my door."

"What?" I stared at her through the goo-goo eyes. "What sort of a love-poem-y thing?"

"Oh, a few lines from the play."

"How do you know it was from Liam? I mean, did he sign his name?"

"No, but it was Romeo talking about being banished. Which Liam is, poor muppet. Willow says he's doing props with Miss Bluestone now. How awful. I should probably reach out to him."

"No," I said too fast. "I mean, what for?"

"Because he's obviously pining for me, the dimwit. Ooh, there's Mr. Torres. Give me back the glasses, quick!"

I handed her the glasses; she put them on crooked. "Hullo, Mr. Torres. Can this be my costume ball mask, please?"

He guffawed. "Yes, but only for today."

The other cast members streamed into the auditorium— Willow, Ajay, Keisha, Lucy, and a bunch of kids who were servants and dancers. The costume party was such a big and complicated scene that Mr. Torres had brought three Tupperwares of cookies that day, which everyone attacked as if they hadn't tasted chocolate chips since preschool.

But not me. My brain was spinning. Gemma didn't think I'd written the note: That was good. But now I'd sent her to "reach out" to Liam: That was bad.

And what if she mentioned the love-poem-y note, and he swore he hadn't written it? She'd immediately know it was me, the other Romeo—and just now I'd pretended it *wasn't*, thereby making the whole thing even WORSE.

Of course, I couldn't have told her the truth, any-way, not if she thought Liam was stupid for sending her a "love-poem-y thing." What was so stupid about it, any-way? It bothered me that she thought it was, considering I'd spent forever finding the perfect words.

The scene began. Lord Capulet gives the servants instructions and flirts with his guests. Tybalt spies Romeo and gets angry that Capulet's party has been crashed by a repulsive Montague. Romeo sees Juliet for the first time; he says a short speech and weaves his way through the dancing guests to her side.

So there I was, standing in front of Gemma. Who was wearing the googly eyeglasses.

I blanked.

"If I profane with my unworthiest hand," Miss Bluestone prompted me.

I nodded. "If I profane with my unworthiest hand this holy shrine, the gentle fine is this . . ."

"My lips," Miss Bluestone said.

"My lips, two blushing pilgrims, ready stand to smooth that, um . . ."

"Rough touch."

"Rough touch with—dang!"

Gemma giggled. "Shall I take off my mask? I think it's distracting you, Mattie."

I nodded. I wiped the sweat off my face with the back of my hand.

She took off the glasses and looked into my eyes. Looking into hers, I could see that her irises were ringed with a darker shade. It was like an eclipse. Solar or lunar? I couldn't remember.

I wiped my face again.

"To smooth that rough touch," Miss Bluestone said. She fluttered her hand.

"To smooth that rough touch," I repeated.

"With a tender kiss."

"With a—"

Before I could finish, Gemma smooched my mouth.

Then she laughed. "Come on, Mats, that wasn't so awful, was it?"

I shook my head. It just made me feel dizzier.

Juliet says a few more lines. Then Romeo speaks, then Juliet, back and forth, while my knees were shaking.

Two more kisses to go. I can do this.

"Then move not, while my prayer's effect I take," I said. "Thus from my lips, by yours, my sin is purged."

I leaned in to kiss her.

"Woo," someone shouted. "Go, Mattie."

Ajay? It could have been. Other people were laughing.

"None of that," Mr. Torres snapped. "This is hard."

"Yes, it's very challenging to kiss *me*," Gemma said, giggling.

"I'm serious," Mr. Torres continued, glaring at the cast members in the audience. "No sounds. No jokes. Total silence. Understood?"

He was so mad he didn't even call them "humans."

"All right, let's pick it up from Juliet's line," Mr. Torres said.

"Then have my lips the sin that they have took," Gemma said.

"Sin from thy lips?" I began.

"No, Mattie," Miss Bluestone called out in exasperation. "The line is 'sin from *my* lips.'"

230 ⁂ BARBARA DEE

"Sorry. Sin from my lips? O trespass sweetly urged! Um . . ."

"Give me my sin again," Gemma whispered.

"Gemma, let Miss Bluestone do the cuing, please," Mr. Torres said.

"Give me my sin again," Miss Bluestone said in a swoony-actressy sort of voice.

Someone in the audience giggled. It could have been Tessa.

Mr. Torres's face reddened.

"Give me my sin again," I said quickly. Then I kissed Gemma.

And before I could get myself offstage, I collapsed.

32

"I'll tell thee ere thou ask it me again."
— *Romeo and Juliet*, II.iii.48

It wasn't a true faint, like when book heroines black out and sprawl on the floor. But I did sink to my knees with a buzzing head. So immediately, Mr. Torres, Tessa, and Lucy ran to my side.

"It's nothing," Lucy was saying loudly. "Mattie does this all the time. She has a very, very sensitive—"

"Stomach," Tessa finished. "We're lucky she didn't barf."

"Shouldn't we call a parent?" Miss Bluestone asked, hovering.

"No," I said. "I'll be fine. I just need a minute." I tried to stand up, but I swayed a little, clutching Tessa's arm.

"I'll get some water. And some damp towels," Lucy said, running out of the auditorium.

"Mattie, put your head between your knees," Mr. Torres said. "Here, sit on this chair."

I did. It made me feel stupid and helpless, but also less queasy.

A minute later Lucy was back with a bottle of water and some wet paper towels, which she put on my forehead and my neck. Cold water was dripping down my face and my back, causing my T-shirt to stick to my skin.

"I'm feeling much better," I announced.

"Good," Mr. Torres said, looking unsure. "I hope it wasn't my wife's cookies."

"Oh, no. I didn't even eat any. I think it just may be a stomach bug or something."

"It better not be, because I'll get it too," Gemma said, smiling a little.

I drank some water and walked around the stage for a few minutes. Then we continued the scene. Romeo had almost nothing left to say, and zero kissing, so it went fine.

But I couldn't wait to get home, crochet some cute baby animals, and hide under my covers.

The next day, Friday, was the balcony scene.

"You're feeling up for it today?" Tessa asked me at lunch.

"I have to," I said grimly. "I have no choice."

Tessa frowned. "I just don't get why you're so nervous, all of a sudden."

Lucy and I exchanged glances.

I nodded.

Tessa deserved to know. It was time.

"Remember that crush I had?" I murmured. "I still have it."

"Okay," Tessa said. "And?"

"That's why the scene was hard for me."

Tessa stared.

I nodded.

Her mouth dropped open. "You mean it's . . . ?"

"Gemma," I said. "Exactly."

"Oh. Okay. Whoa."

"Yep."

"I had no idea. Really? So does this mean you—"

"It just means I like her. That's *all* it means, Tessa. Please don't tell anybody else, okay?"

Tessa's face reddened. "Of course I wouldn't! You think I go around talking behind your back, Mattie?"

"No, no." Now I was blushing too. "I just want to be super careful. Especially at school."

"Mattie, at theater camp I knew a *bunch* of kids who are gay. Like my good friend Henry, for example! You think I'm incapable of respecting privacy?"

"Volume control," I said, pointing to my mouth.

"Eep. Sorry." She leaned toward me. "But I don't understand this, anyway. If she's your crush, shouldn't you *want* to kiss her?"

I winced. "Not in public. Onstage. With all these people watching and laughing, and Miss Bluestone correcting."

"Mattie, why don't you ask Mr. Torres if you can just leave out the kissing?" Lucy said.

"Because it's *Romeo and Juliet*! They get married! They *die* for each other! What are we supposed to do instead—fist-bump?"

"Good point," Tessa said. "Kissing is absolutely required. And since there's all this secrecy, I take it Gemma doesn't know?"

I shook my head.

"Unclear," Lucy blurted. "Mattie sent Gemma a note."

I glared at her. We hadn't agreed to keep the note a secret from Tessa, but it was my information to share, not Lucy's.

Tessa blinked at Lucy. "You knew all about this, didn't you?"

Lucy blushed. "Yes, but not because Mattie told me. I just sort of . . . figured it out."

"And then you came rushing to share it with me. So loyal of you, Lucy."

"Tessa, it wasn't up to me!"

"I asked Lucy to keep it to herself," I said. "I needed time to, you know . . ."

"*Think* about it?" Tessa's mouth twisted. For a second, I thought she might start crying, but she didn't. Even so, I felt awful for leaving her out. Why did something good have to end up hurting people?

Lucy and I exchanged a helpless glance.

"Anyway," Tessa said after a minute or two, "do you guys plan on telling me *about* this note?"

"It was while you were away last week," I said. I told her the whole story, including Gemma's interpretation.

"Oh, great," Tessa said. "So now Gemma's going to 'reach out' to Liam? I bet that means she'll ask him to the Valentine's Dance."

"If Willow hasn't already," Lucy said.

"Aww, thanks. That makes me feel *so* much better." Tessa chomped on a potato chip. "Mattie, you told me Gemma didn't even *like* Liam."

My stomach clenched. "I said she thought he was a dim muppet. But now she feels sorry for him, I guess."

"Well, this is all going swimmingly. Maybe the three of us can just go to the stupid dance together. *What?*" she added, when she realized I was giving Lucy a look.

"There's something else you don't know, Tessa," Lucy said. "I asked Elijah. To the dance."

"Elijah Dirtbag? You *didn't*."

"No, I did. It was kind of a mix-up, but I asked him, and he said yes."

"That's insane. *You're* insane. Holy crap. Anything *else* I need to know?"

"No, that about covers it," I said.

"So I'm finally all caught up, then? Well, woohoo." Suddenly, Tessa reached into her bag and flung a handful of chips at us.

Lucy squealed. "What's *that* for?"

"Keeping secrets from me, you false caterpillars. Luckily for you both, I have a *ridiculously* forgiving heart. Which neither of you two scurvy knaves deserve. *Incoming*," she added, lifting her chin.

I spun around to see Gemma walking toward our table, with Willow and Isabel lagging behind her. Quickly, I brushed off the potato chip shards.

Gemma, unlike the other two, looked concerned. "Hullo, Mattie. How are you feeling today?"

"Great," I said. "It was probably just a twenty-four-hour thingy."

"Oh, I hope so. Well, good to hear you're better. See you later, then." She smiled at Tessa and Lucy, and squeezed my shoulder. Willow and Isabel turned their backs without saying a word, and the three of them left.

"Seriously, Mattie, you should just tell her," Tessa said. "Although, if you ask me, she already knows."

"O, I am Fortune's fool!"
—*Romeo and Juliet*, III.i.138

Do not pass out.

Do not mess up.

Do not pass out.

Do not mess up.

I recited these lines to myself all afternoon, determined not to screw up the balcony scene. Everything should be easier, anyway, I told myself. Because it would just be Gemma and me in the auditorium—plus Mr. Torres and Miss Bluestone. Fewer eyes on us. No giggles or hoots.

Plus, there was an extremely weird thing I'd noticed: The most famous love scene ever written for the stage didn't have a single kiss in it. It was all words. But words I could handle. If I was good at anything, it was Shakespeare's words.

When I got to the auditorium, Mr. Torres walked over

to me immediately. "You're sure you're up for this today, Mattie? No more dizzy spells?"

"I'm fine, Mr. Torres! But thanks!"

"Okay, but you'll tell me if you start to feel woozy?"

"Promise," I said.

We waited a few minutes for Gemma to show, but she was late again. Mr. Torres didn't even try to hide his annoyance as he checked his watch. Finally, he told me to start without her; the scene opens with a long speech by Romeo, anyway.

Which I nailed. The whole speech. Didn't miss a word.

The way Mr. Torres beamed at me, I felt like teacher's pet all over again. And from the back of the auditorium, someone shouted, "Brava!"

It was Gemma. She practically danced down the aisle. "That was perfect, Mattie! Well done! Full marks!"

"You were here the whole time?" I tried to sound nonchalant as she climbed onstage.

She nodded, laughing. "I thought if I hid it might help you focus! And I was right! So all you have to do from now on is imagine I'm invisible, and you'll be fine!"

Sure. No problem. Easy peasy.

"All right, humans, let's keep the momentum going," Mr. Torres said. "Gemma, you're up. *O Romeo, Romeo, wherefore art thou*, et cetera."

Gemma said the lines as if she'd written them herself. And I—I mean Romeo—answered. We had a conversation. Back and forth. It was going great.

Until Gemma held up her hand and asked for time, as if this were a soccer match.

"Mr. Torres, don't you think it's odd that there's no physical contact at all between Romeo and Juliet in this scene? Considering what's happening onstage?"

"Yes," I said quickly, before Mr. Torres could answer. "I noticed it too. But Shakespeare is very specific about when he wants kisses. So I don't think we should just plop some in."

Mr. Torres nodded. "I agree, Mattie. But Gemma has a point—it might look funny if all they do is *talk* at each other the whole scene. How about this—Romeo, you lean in several times as if you *want* to kiss Juliet, but Juliet, you always pull back. Can we try that?"

"Sure, let's," Gemma said eagerly.

Do not mess up. Do not pass out. Do not mess up—

I started chanting to myself again. And maybe because of chanting and the leaning in and the possibility that Gemma had used a new shampoo that smelled like hyacinths, which happened to be my favorite flower scent of all, I messed up my lines. A whole bunch of times: Twice by tripping over the consonants. Once by saying the wrong speech. Three times by saying the right words in the wrong order. Five times by drawing a complete blank.

When we finished the scene. Gemma smiled at me with soft eyes. "It'll be okay, Mattie. You just need to relax."

"Yeah," I said, watching Miss Bluestone say something to Mr. Torres that involved holding her hands in front of her as if she were shaking an imaginary coconut, and Mr. Torres hanging his head and not answering.

I felt exactly like a dried-up slug. I couldn't even look at Gemma, though I felt her eyes still on me as she put on her jacket and called out a good-bye.

When she'd left the auditorium, and Miss Bluestone finally stopped shaking her coconut, I walked over to Mr. Torres, who was typing into his phone.

He looked up at me, and I noticed that the shadows under his eyes were back.

"Hey, Mattie," he said quietly. "What's up?"

I couldn't tell if the question meant: *What's wrong with you, anyway?* But that's the question I chose to answer.

"Mr. Torres, I'm not sure I can do this anymore," I said.

"You mean the play?"

I nodded.

"What's going on? You said Romeo's speech beautifully before Gemma came onstage. When we were just reading through the scenes together in my classroom, you had no trouble, and I know you have no problem memorizing—"

"It's not that."

"No? Then what is it?"

"I can't really . . . talk about it."

He sighed. I could see he was frustrated with me, and trying not to show it. "Mattie, I can't help you if you don't communicate."

"I know! I'm just not comfortable explaining it!"

"Is it Gemma?"

My stomach dropped. Omigod, so it was that obvious. "What do you mean?"

He studied my face for a few too many seconds. "Are you girls not getting along?"

"No, no, we're getting along great! I'm just . . . distracted."

"By what?"

"Gemma." My face burned, but the rest of my body broke out in a chilly sweat.

Mr. Torres scratched his nose. "Well, I don't know what to tell you, Mattie. You're obviously feeling stuff right now that's getting in your way onstage. So I'm wondering if somehow you can *use* whatever you're feeling in your acting."

"How would I do *that*?"

"Come on, Mattie," Mr. Torres said kindly. "You're a

great reader. And you know that feeling when you're reading a book, and you're totally connected to the character? It almost feels as if you're thinking the same thoughts."

"Yeah." It happened to me all the time, in fact.

"Listen, I'm not saying you're the same as Romeo. Far from it! But think about this: Romeo is like you because he's feeling something deeply that he can't express in public, right?"

I didn't say anything. I couldn't.

"So if you can somehow channel whatever *you're* feeling to Romeo's love for Juliet, which he has to keep private from his family and his friends, it might help you connect with his character. Who knows, it might even help you deal with your *own* emotions."

I swallowed. "Maybe."

"Because otherwise I'm not sure we can go on," Mr. Torres said. "You're the only one who can play Romeo at this point. If you can't find a way to continue, no one will step into your shoes. We'll just have to cancel the production."

"Couldn't you be Romeo? Instead of me?" I begged.

"No," Mr. Torres said firmly. "That wouldn't be appropriate, given the material. This is an eighth-grade production, so Romeo has to be an eighth grader." Then his voice softened. "Mattie, look: I know playing this role was never your plan, so if you really don't have it in you, that's okay. We'll just do a talent show or something. It'll be fine."

I shook my head. "I don't know!"

"What don't you know?"

"What I want to do! About any of it!"

"All right," he said quietly after a minute. "So why don't you do some thinking this weekend? And then stop by my homeroom on Monday morning, and we'll see where we are."

❀34❀

"One too many by my weary self."
—*Romeo and Juliet*, I.i.131

On Saturday morning, Kayden yanked me out of a dream. It was a nice dream about being on a beach, except I was being bitten by a swarm of mosquitoes. And when I tried to swat them away, I felt my little brother pinching my arm.

"Wakeupwakeupwakeup," he was chanting.

"Erg. What time is it?"

"Ten thirty."

"On a Saturday? And you woke me *up*?"

"Mom says you sleep too much."

"Too much for what?"

"And Dad made bacon."

"Woohoo, bacon."

"Also, someone's here."

"Yeah? Like who?"

"I don't remember. She talks funny. She said she's in the play with you."

I bolted upright. *"Gemma?"*

Kayden nodded. "She's eating the bacon."

"Tell her to come up to my room. No—first let me brush my teeth, *then* tell her to come up. What's wrong with you, Kayden? Why didn't you tell me right away?"

"You were sleeping," he explained.

I shooed him out of my room. *Gemma* was here? In my house? What for?

I brushed my teeth and splashed cold water on my face. Then I threw on my robe and ran downstairs to the kitchen.

There she was, calmly eating bacon and scrambled eggs. Mom and Dad were drinking coffee and reading the newspaper. Mason was pouring chocolate milk into his cereal.

"Good morning, sleepyhead," Dad greeted me. "We've been chatting with your costar."

Gemma flashed a smile. "Hullo, Mattie. I've eaten all your breakfast, I'm afraid."

"That's okay, I never eat breakfast on Saturdays," I said.

"It's true, she doesn't," Mason said. "She always just sleeps until lunch."

"Not true, doofus," I grumbled. I looked at Mom, but she was doing the crossword puzzle. Was somebody going to explain to me what was going on?

Apparently, no.

I poured myself some coffee.

"You drink coffee at breakfast?" Gemma asked me. "Daddy forbids it, but I always have tea, anyway."

Mom looked up from her puzzle. "Oh, would you like some tea, dear? We have Earl Grey."

Gemma blushed. "Thank you, Mrs. Monaghan, I've already had some at home. I was just saying."

"Who's Earl Grey?" Mason demanded.

"Probably nobody," Dad said. "Although I do think there was an actual Earl of Sandwich. And that's where we get the word for 'sandwich.'" He smiled at Gemma, as if she, being English, would appreciate this factoid.

"You mean sandwiches are named after some dude named *Earl*?" Mason guffawed. Chocolate milk dribbled out of the side of his mouth.

This was now officially unbearable.

"Gemma, let's go upstairs, okay?" I said, pretending there was no rule in my house that hot beverages weren't allowed outside the kitchen.

Gemma stood. "Well, thank you so much for the delicious breakfast, Mrs. Monaghan."

"Anytime, dear," Mom said, smiling sweetly as she filled in a crossword answer.

We walked upstairs, me dripping some coffee on the

carpet and not caring. When we got upstairs to my room, I shut the door.

"So what's up?" I asked, realizing I sounded like Mr. Torres. Except I wasn't asking what was *wrong* with Gemma; I was asking why she was *here*.

"May I sit?" she asked.

I snatched my wool and crochet stuff off my beanbag chair and motioned for her to sit there.

"Cute," she said, examining the tiny blue dolphin.

"Thanks. It's just a hobby." Inwardly, I rolled my eyes. Because *of course* it was just a hobby. You couldn't crochet baby animals for a *job*.

Gemma smiled at my polka-dot curtains and my butterfly mobile. "You have a very pretty room, Mattie. It isn't how I expected it."

"How did you expect it?"

"I don't know. More mysterious."

"Huh," I said. "You mean like black walls?"

"Oh, yes." She laughed. "And fuzzy purple creatures popping out of your desk."

So she thought of me as freakish. *Hey, great.*

My hand trembled as I sipped my coffee. "Can I ask why you're here, Gemma? Not to be rude or anything."

"Oh, of course. It's a fair question." She chewed her lower lip. "Mattie, I wanted to ask you something. In person."

My heart zoomed. "You do? What?"

"It's kind of awkward. But . . ." She searched my face. "Okay, I'll just say it. Do you want to be Romeo?"

"What?" It wasn't the question I'd been expecting. Or, rather, hoping for. "What do you mean?"

"I mean, Willow thinks you don't. So she's been asking Liam to be Romeo again. She's been asking him nonstop since he broke his arm."

"Okay," I said, to show I was listening.

"At first he said no. But lately he's been feeling terrible about leaving the play. Working on props with Miss Bluestone is ghastly, apparently, and he feels as if everyone's forgotten about him."

"So he wants his job back? As Romeo?"

"He says he's willing to give it a go."

"But Liam can't even memorize his phone number!"

"He can tape some lines to his cast, he says. Mr. Torres told him he could when he broke his arm."

"He can't tape the whole play! And why is this Willow's business, anyway?"

Gemma shrugged. "She likes Liam."

"And she hates *me*, although I've never done anything to deserve it."

"She doesn't hate you, Mattie," Gemma said gently. "She's just not your friend."

I sighed. As much as that explanation annoyed me, as much as it made no sense, I could see that it was probably true. "Gemma, what do you want me to say?"

"I want you to say that you *do* want to be Romeo. Because *I* want you to be."

"Really?"

Gemma nodded. "Nothing against Liam. He's adorable and gorgeous, and it was so sweet how he put that love-poem-y thing under my door. I even asked him to the Valentine's Dance, as a way of saying thank you for it."

Oh, perfect. Well played, Mattie.

"However," she added, "he's a terrible actor. You're so much better at it, Mattie."

"But that's not true! I keep messing up my lines—"

"Because you get distracted. When you focus, you're brilliant."

I blushed. "Thank you."

"You're welcome. Although there's more."

I stared at her, barely breathing.

"Willow wants me to tell Mr. Torres that I agree with her, that I also think Liam should take back Romeo. From you."

"And will you?"

"No," Gemma said. "Not if you want Romeo."

"I think I do," I blurted.

Her face colored. She beamed. "Yes! I was hoping you'd say that!"

She got up from the beanbag chair, threw her arms around me, kissed my cheek, and left.

When Monday rolled around, I went straight to Mr. Torres's homeroom and announced that I'd decided to keep playing Romeo. He grinned and said he'd never doubted it. I couldn't tell if Willow had already come to him with her plan to have me replaced, but when I saw Mr. Torres's reaction to my announcement, I knew he'd never take the role from me.

So I stopped worrying about it. I even told Gemma.

"He's ace, isn't he?" she said. But it's not like it was a question.

❀ 35 ❀

"Now the two hours' traffic
of our stage."
—*Romeo and Juliet*, Prologue, 12

The next few weeks flew by. Rehearsals lasted from dismissal to dinner, and sometimes beyond when we were getting measured for costumes or adjusting lights, or if the scenery needed repairing. The PTA sent us pizzas when we were running late, and Mom even brought over some home-baked cupcakes for us one evening. Which was really nice of her, especially because she wasn't a cupcake-baking sort of mom.

As for me, I messed up my lines only a few more times after Gemma's visit. It still made me swimmy-headed whenever we had to kiss (five times over the entire play!), but I tried to "use" that feeling the way Mr. Torres suggested, telling myself that Romeo probably felt swimmy-headed too. And somehow, knowing that both Gemma and Mr.

Torres believed in me, were rooting for me, helped me to relax a little. Never totally, but enough for me to remember all my lines. And to focus on my character.

Finally, we were down to the last few days before opening night. That Wednesday, Willow's mom and Isabel's mom showed up with all of our costumes. We couldn't all try on our outfits in the bathroom, so Mr. Torres had the boys go to a first-floor classroom, and Miss Bluestone led all the girls to the gym.

"All right, young ladies," Miss Bluestone said. "Let me explain how the costumes work. All Montagues are in shades of blue, and all Capulets are in shades of red. Most of you will have one outfit. Certain characters, like Benvolio, Mercutio, and Lady Capulet, may have an additional accessory— for example, a scarf or a shawl—to wear in some scenes, so we're asking you to keep track of all items. Our leads"—she beamed at Gemma and me—"have multiple costumes, and will have assistants backstage to help them dress."

Gemma, who was standing next to Willow, flashed me a look like, *Ooh, posh!*

I grinned.

Willow's mom came over to me. "Mattie, quick question: What were you planning to do with your hair?"

"My hair? You mean, for the play?" Stupidly, I hadn't given it any thought.

"You really should get a haircut, Mattie," Willow said. "If you're playing Romeo."

"Oh no, you *mustn't*," Gemma exclaimed. "Mattie, you have such gorgeous hair. Don't you *dare* trim it one inch!"

"Well, she can't just wear it like *that*!" Willow pointed at my hair, which hung messily down my back. "It's too long and girly. It'll confuse the audience."

Charlotte sniggered. "Yeah, *Romea and Juliet*."

I froze. I couldn't look at Gemma, but I could feel her eyes on me.

Then Tessa came to my rescue. "Hey, Mattie, just put it up in a man-bun. That'll definitely look Shakespearey."

"They had man-buns then?" Charlotte scrunched her face in disbelief.

Tessa nodded. "Oh, yes. I took a class in theater camp called Shakespeare's Costumes. Also, the actors wore earrings. And tights!"

When Willow's mom turned her back to locate my costumes, I asked Tessa if she was sure about the man-bun.

"Nah," she admitted, grinning. "I just made that up. But Gemma likes your hair, so you *can't* cut it, right?"

I hugged her. "Thanks, Tessa."

"You're welcome, saucy wench."

A few minutes later I was wearing my first costume, which was basically just a blue tunic with a wide leather belt, and black leggings. The funny thing was, I felt a twinge of disappointment, because maybe this wasn't costumey *enough*.

But Gemma's costume was amazing, a long scarlet dress with puffy sleeves and a square neckline. Everyone was making a fuss over how beautiful she looked: the teachers, all the girls—and then, when we were back onstage with everyone, the boys.

This was like a kick in the stomach, watching Liam walk over to her and do a joke bow. Followed by Gemma curtsying, and then the two of them pretending to waltz around the stage, until they crashed into Ajay. I wondered if Tessa found this as painful to watch as I did—a reminder that Liam and Gemma were going together to the dance. I hadn't mentioned this fact to Tessa, but she probably knew, because everyone was keeping a scorecard of dance couples.

Also, I wondered if Liam felt weird seeing Lucy pretend sword-fighting with Elijah in his monk costume. Maybe by now Liam had fallen out of crush with Lucy, the way Romeo had with Rosaline. And the way I had with Elijah. Even if Liam had forgotten about Lucy, I should tell Lucy how he'd wanted to ask her to the dance.

But sometime later, after all this was over.

* * *

If you wait a long time for something, you can start to believe it will never happen. And then when it finally does happen, you're shocked.

That's how I felt when opening night arrived. The whole day, I kept thinking: *Really? Now we're actually* doing *this play, not just practicing?* My whole body zinged with electricity, like you could use me for a Christmas decoration. I couldn't stop jiggling my feet and tapping my fingers. Even Tessa scolded me ("Mattie: Calm down, breathe, focus.")

She also made me eat a banana ("for energy") and drink water an hour before curtain, even though I swore I wasn't hungry or thirsty.

"Mattie, listen to me," she said. "It's a looong play, and you're like an athlete about to run a marathon."

Which turned out to be the opposite of how it felt. It was like we'd entered another dimension, where time was different. Because all the weeks of practicing had led us to a two-hour performance that somehow was over in a flash.

And yet I can still remember every detail: Benvolio teasing Romeo about his crush on Rosaline. The Nurse teasing Juliet. Tybalt strutting around the costume ball. Mercutio's Queen Mab speech (which Tessa nailed). Lord Capulet threatening to throw Juliet out of the house when she refused to marry Paris.

There were surprises. Some lines that had never seemed funny in rehearsal got big laughs from the audience, like when Romeo is listening to Juliet on the balcony, and he asks, "Shall I hear more, or shall I speak at this?" Also, when Tybalt stabs Mercutio, and Mercutio makes stupid jokes—I'd never realized before how angry Mercutio was. But I guess Tessa had saved her anger for the performance, because when she said the line "A plague o' both your houses," she actually spat. I mean, with *actual spit*.

As for me, I messed up only once, at the end of the play. It happened when Juliet awakens in the vault, sees Romeo lying dead beside her, and kisses his lips to get the poison he'd swallowed. In rehearsals, all of my kisses with Gemma were quick little pecks, but this time she took an extra second. And I guess I was thrown by that, because without thinking, I opened my eyes. Not so wide that anyone in the audience laughed, or probably even noticed—but just wide enough that Gemma saw me looking at her.

It wasn't about me, I knew. But still.

When we finished, there was a standing ovation. People yelled, "Bravo," and "Brava" and made us come back onstage for extra bows—the whole cast, and then specifically Gemma and me. Just before our curtain call, Gemma reached up to pull all the bobby pins out of my man-bun.

"Let them see you," she whispered.

So during our final bows, I looked like myself, Mattie Monaghan. And Gemma glowed at me.

Then Mr. Torres joined us onstage. "Hello, parents and friends of the eighth grade! We want to thank you for supporting us as we mounted our most ambitious show ever. In the history of our eighth-grade productions, we've never before staged a nearly unabridged Shakespeare play, so I'm beyond proud of our efforts this year. It wasn't easy, and I have to admit that at times it seemed impossible. But as I told one of our brightest stars here"—*he gestured to ME!*—"a teacher never bets against his students. So I always knew we were capable of something special tonight—and I think you'll agree that I was right!"

Booming applause. A pretty dark-haired woman who had to be Mrs. Torres came to the edge of the stage to hand a bouquet to Mr. Torres, who held it to his chest and mouthed, *I love you.* Everybody went, "Awwww."

Afterward, in the faculty lounge we'd taken over for our dressing room, Lucy, Tessa, and I had a laughing, crying, sweaty friend-hug. Keisha, Ellie, and Elijah joined us, and Mr. Torres gave the six of us high fives. Then we all joined our families in the audience.

"Little sister, you rocked," shouted Cara, who'd driven all the way from school for the performance. "Not that I predicted it, or anything!"

"You were absolutely great," Mom said, beaming through her mom tears. Dad kissed my cheek; his eyes were red, I saw.

"I liked the fighting with the swords," Kayden said. "But why did you get in the middle of Tessa and that other girl?"

"I didn't—*Romeo* did," I tried to explain. "He's not the same as me."

But this was a kid who thought *Star Wars* was real. So I left it at that.

"Gemma! Congratulations!" Dad boomed.

I turned. Gemma had joined us, along with her dad and a chic woman wearing too much makeup. Gemma's mom, I realized immediately. They had the same heart-shaped face.

"Congratulations to Mattie," Gemma shouted. "My Romeo!"

She kissed my cheek.

Everyone laughed.

Even (and this was the funny part) me. Even though the play we'd just performed was a tragedy. Even though I'd probably never get to hang out with Gemma again. Even though I'd never told her how I felt.

I laughed. And for the rest of that night, I couldn't stop smiling.

36

"This night I hold an old-accustom'd feast,
Whereto I have invited many a guest,
Such as I love."
—*Romeo and Juliet*, I.ii. 20–22

Word got out overnight that Willow was hosting a cast party at her house on Saturday evening, and everyone from the play was invited—everyone except Tessa and me.

At seven on Saturday morning, Tessa texted me: *RAT-CATCHER! SCURVY KNAVE!! We should totally crash it, Mattie!!!*

I was too excited to sleep late, so I texted back: *Nope. Just come over tonight, kay?*

Tessa: *but how can Willow be such a MONSTROUS MALEFACTOR?*

Me: *It's her party. Her house. A plague on it :P*

Tessa: *but everyone from the play will be there!!!*

Me: *If they want to go, let them. Who cares?*

Tessa: *me. i care :(*

Did I? It was strange to realize that I didn't. Not even a little. I knew Willow didn't like me any more than she had before the play, and probably I'd never know the reason why. Maybe she thought I was nerdy or stuck-up. Maybe she thought I was stealing Gemma from her, or had stolen Romeo from Liam. Or maybe she just didn't like my eyebrows. Or my earlobes, or whatever.

As for Willow not inviting Tessa, I have to admit that seemed more logical to me. Tessa was a great person, but it would be easy to find her obnoxious. Sometimes she overdid it with the Shakespeare-insults thing, and even I'd been having trouble with her volume control lately. A team-captain sort of person like Willow wouldn't appreciate anyone who didn't follow orders. And being friends with me was probably not helping Tessa either.

So I asked Mom to drive me over to the grocery store to get chips and soda. Tessa and I were having our own private cast party, I told her.

"What about Lucy?" Mom asked.

I hesitated. Of course I knew that Lucy would be outraged that Tessa and I had been excluded, and would skip Willow's party on principle. But it didn't seem fair for me to invite her over that evening. She had every right to celebrate with the rest of the cast, I thought. She'd earned it.

But when Lucy's mom called mine to arrange a carpool

to Willow's house, Mom told Mrs. Yang why I wasn't going. So, of course, Lucy immediately called my cell to say she refused to go to Willow's, and would tell "everyone" how Willow had purposely left Tessa and me off the guest list.

"You don't have to do that," I protested.

"Oh yes, I do," Lucy answered firmly. "It's about time someone did."

That was the end of it. You didn't argue with Lucy once she'd made a decision.

At six that evening, Tessa showed up at my house with a pint of vanilla ice cream, a bag of smashed Oreos, and a small pack of jelly beans.

At six fifteen, Lucy arrived with Keisha and Ellie. They were carrying trays of homemade brownies.

At six thirty, Elijah rang the doorbell, with Jake and Ajay on the step behind him.

Cara came over to me and whispered, "Turn on some music. I'll run out to get more food and stuff. And pizza."

"Hurry," I said. I was starting to panic a little, because I hadn't hosted a party since my tenth birthday.

It was a good thing she was quick. Because by seven, there were thirteen cast members at my house. By seven thirty, there were twenty-six—including Liam. And before people started leaving around ten o'clock that night, everyone from the play had stopped by—everyone except for Willow, Charlotte, and Isabel.

And Gemma.

I had a good time, I really did, dancing with Liam and Lucy and Keisha—although the fact that Gemma had stayed away was distracting. By now I felt sure that the two of us were good friends despite Willow, although it seemed that Gemma's loyalty to Willow was stronger than her friendship with me. I didn't see any other way to think about her not showing up in my living room.

But at eleven that night, still buzzing from all the sugar and the dance music, I got a text.

Gemma: *Sorry I missed your party!!*

Me: *It wasn't really mine, it was the cast's. You were at Willow's?*

Gemma: *No, had to dine with Mummy then go back to her hotel. Bloody boooring.*

Me: *Oh, too bad.*

Gemma: *Willow had it worse, apparently. Loads of food but no one showed.*

Me: *Whoa, literally no one?*

Gemma: *A few, but sounds like they left almost immediately to go to your house.*

Me: **no comment**

Gemma: **me neither**

37

On Sunday morning, before she made the trip back to college, Cara and I did our French toast ritual. At the diner, we didn't bother with menus. By this time, the waitress remembered our usual orders, but when she started to fill my cup with coffee, Cara pulled it away from me.

"No coffee," she said. "You're so twitchy—the last thing you need is caffeine!"

"But I always drink coffee at breakfast!" I protested.

"Fine. Can she have some decaf, please?" Cara asked the waitress. Then she grinned at me. "Jeez, haven't you heard of post-production letdown?"

"Yeah, sure," I admitted. "But I can't help it if I'm not depressed!"

"No, I guess you can't. Oh, well." She grinned. "So what's next on the school calendar?"

"Nothing. Just school."

"You sure about that?"

The waitress brought my decaf. I dumped a jug of half-and-half into it and took a slurpy sip. "What do you mean?" I asked.

"Remember the Valentine's Dance?"

I rolled my eyes. "Yeah, I guess. But who cares? I'm not going."

"Mattie, you have to."

"Are you serious? Why?"

"Because Mom's in charge of it. She's done a ton of organizing. She'll feel embarrassed if her own daughter doesn't show up."

"Yeah, but I already told her I probably wasn't going. It's not like she doesn't know!"

"She may know, and I'm sure she won't force you. But she'll still feel bad if you don't."

"Cara, why should she?"

"Because she did it for *you*, doofus. To be part of your school. And your *life*."

The waitress brought our French toast at that point, which was lucky, because I wanted to end this conversation.

It really bothered me that my big sister, who was usually so supportive (when she wasn't just talking about herself), was now guilting me about the stupid dance. I'd just had the best two days in my school career, probably the best two days of my *entire life*, and here was Cara telling me I should do something that would make me miserable.

I mean, it would be weird enough watching Elijah and Lucy dancing together. And as for Gemma and Liam? My brain cells refused to even imagine it. I'd totally messed up when it came to this couples business.

But also the whole idea of dress shopping with Mom under time pressure, when I'd sworn I wouldn't ask her to do that—it sounded like the worst possible way to spend my Sunday. And even if I did ask Mom to take me shopping, and even if she did say yes (after giving me a hard time about breaking my promise to her), how would I know what dress to pick out, anyway? It would be like thinking up a costume.

The waitress brought Cara the check. She put some money on the table, then raised an eyebrow at me.

"So?" she said. "Any thoughts about this dance?"

"It's too late, anyway," I grumbled. "It's in a few days, and I haven't asked anyone. And no one's asked me."

"What about Gemma?"

I swallowed. "What about her?"

"I thought she was your crush."

The *no big deal* way she said this almost made me laugh. "Cara, I can't go to the Valentine's Dance *with Gemma*."

"Why not?"

"Because this is middle school, remember? Kids can be jerks."

"Mattie, you can't let your life be run by jerks." Cara mopped up some maple syrup with a piece of French toast. "Oh, whatever. It's eighth grade. Just go with your friends. Next objection."

"I don't have a dress," I sputtered.

"Ahh," she replied, her eyes sparkling.

We got into her car. She started driving toward the highway, in the opposite direction from our house.

"Where are we going?" I asked.

"It's a surprise," she said. "Don't worry, I'll text Mom when we get there."

She turned on her radio and started singing. We drove for a half hour or so, then we got off at the exit for Mantua. I couldn't remember if I'd ever been to this town before, but none of it seemed familiar, I thought, as Cara parked on a street that had cafés and stores with the word "shoppe" on the awnings.

"Come on, little sister," she said, leading me to a "thrift shoppe" called AdVintage.

"What *is* this place?" I murmured, breathing in a spicy dried-flower smell as we entered.

"This is where you shop when you're an interesting person," Cara declared. "And I am proud to say you now qualify."

She walked over to a rack and held up a black satin dress that looked very 1950s, with a red belt and red buttons. "Whoa. Check out *this*."

"It's very dramatic," I said. "But—"

"And look at all these!"

More dresses. Racks and racks, most of them costumey, really. Except they'd actually been worn as real dresses by real women once. I tried to imagine those wearers, their names and occupations. Lila the advertising executive. Maggie the hat-shop owner. Hortense the rat-catcher.

One dress seemed to me like a Juliet. Not like a Gemma, just a Juliet. It was dark purple velvet, with an open square neck and a full, swingy skirt that would be incredible for dancing.

What was her occupation? Wait—I had it: Juliet the actress.

I tried it on in front of the mirror. I twirled.

"I really love this one," I admitted.

Cara grinned. "Then it's my present to you."

"Really? What for?"

"A rock-star performance in the play," she said. "And also for making Mom happy."

The whole ride home, I thought how weird it was that Cara cared about Mom's feelings so much. Because it seemed that all she ever did was fight with Mom, about everything. Or else complain about Mom's ridiculous standards. Sometimes I even wondered why she came home from college as often as she did, since every visit was usually one long argument.

Finally, as we were pulling into town, I had to ask, "Cara, why do you care if Mom would be upset that I didn't go to this dance?"

"Why do I *care*? What's that supposed to mean?"

"I mean, you don't get along with her. All you two do is fight."

"We have our disagreements, yeah. So?"

"So, do you even *like* her?"

"That's an obnoxious question!"

"Sorry. But do you?"

"I love her, you moron. Mom's the best."

"Seriously?"

"Mattie," Cara said. "Let me tell you something. Whenever I have a boyfriend problem or a roommate problem, who do you think is the first person I talk to?

Mom. Because she's a great listener. She knows me better than anyone. And she loves me."

I couldn't believe what I was hearing. "So why do you fight so much, then?"

Cara laughed. "That's just how it is with us. It has nothing to do with *love*. And one day, when you're ready to talk to her about Gemma or anything else, you'll see all this for yourself."

"I guess," I said.

"You will. But until then, you'd better keep talking to me."

❀ 38 ❀

"Come, musicians, play. / A hall, a hall!
Give room! And foot it, girls!"
Romeo and Juliet, I.v.27–28

I did go to the Valentine's Dance in the Juliet dress. But that Friday night was freezing, and I realized that the dress, with its big, open neckline, would probably feel too light for our school's drafty gym. So I borrowed the Darth Vader cape from my brothers.

"You'd better bring it home with you," Kayden warned me.

"Affirmative," I said, saluting.

Mom didn't drive me, because she needed to be at the gym extra early to set up the snack tables and the disco ball and all that sort of stuff. Before she took off, though, she looked me over.

"Beautiful," she said. "And I'm glad you didn't cut your hair."

"You are?"

"Although your bangs do need another trim." She kissed my forehead.

"Mom?" I said. "Thanks for doing this dance. I know how busy you are."

She seemed shocked I'd said that. So was I, truthfully.

"Well, it's my pleasure," she answered. "But I'm never too busy for my girl. You know that, right?"

I nodded. "And sorry if I've been acting weird lately."

She smiled and brushed my bangs with her fingers. "You haven't been weird, honey. You've been right on schedule."

About a half hour later, Tessa's mom drove over to get me. Tessa was wearing a pale blue sparkly dress that had a Glinda the Good Witch sort of look to it. She even had glitter in her hair somehow.

"You need a wand," I told her.

"Voilà," she said, waving a paper towel roll at me.

By the time we arrived, the gym was full of eighth graders. Most of the girls were in glammy party dresses. The boys were more random—some in suits and ties, some in normal clothes, some in stupid football jerseys. But at least none of them were dressed like zombies this time.

"Omigod, look at Lucy," Tessa shouted over the music. She pointed to the center of the floor, where our quiet, sane friend was doing wild dance moves we'd never even seen before. Elijah was staring at her in awe, as a bunch of people were crowded around them both, cheering.

And then my eye caught Gemma and Liam. They were dancing together—in a way that made them seem as if they *were* together. For real. Both of them so gorgeous (although Gemma was wearing a school outfit, one of her clashing-pattern ensembles), and smiling at each other, as if they were sharing a private joke.

I couldn't watch.

Because really, it was thanks to me that they were together. If I'd told Gemma I'd sent the Romeo note, she wouldn't have asked Liam. And if I hadn't lied to Liam about Lucy, he'd have asked Lucy instead. This whole disaster was due to me, due to lying. Or not lying, exactly: just not telling everyone the truth. Which ended up as bad as lying. So now I was as miserable as I deserved.

"I'm going to get some soda," I told Tessa.

She clutched my arm. "You're leaving me here?"

"No. I just want soda."

"Well, hurry back. Oh, shoot. Incoming." She lifted her chin.

Ajay, of all people, was walking toward us.

"Hello," he said, staring at our feet. "You look nice. Want to dance?"

Tessa and I exchanged glances and burst into giggles.

"Which *one* of us, you mad mustachio purple-hued malt-worm?" she demanded.

He looked up. "You," he told her.

She turned red. "Oh."

They both stood there.

"Okay, time for soda," I announced.

By the time I'd poured some Coke into a paper cup with a heart pattern, they were on the dance floor together. I guess it surprised me that Ajay was a decent dancer—although what really surprised me was how happy Tessa looked. Had she had a secret crush on Ajay all this time—a crush she didn't tell us about because she thought we wouldn't understand? I supposed it was possible. Anything was, when it came to crushes, really.

I grabbed a few chips and a red napkin cut into a heart shape. Mom had clearly worked overtime on all the Valentine-themey details: there were heart-shaped balloons and heart-shaped cupcakes, little cellophane bundles of chocolate kisses, and all the tables, covered in red paper, had plastic vases with red silk roses.

I found a chair on the sidelines next to some kids who'd been in the tech crew. I could see Mom across the floor chatting with Mr. Torres, who was chaperoning. Maybe there was some mother-daughter telepathy thing going on, because at that exact moment, Mom smiled at me and waved.

I smiled and waved back, causing the cape to slip off my shoulder.

She pointed at me, mouthing the word, *Beautiful*.

I held up the heart-shaped napkin and pointed to her. Maybe I *could* talk to my mom sometime, I thought— about Gemma and everything else. Because if Cara could, so could I, right? After all, Cara was way more difficult. And prickly. And if she thought Mom not only listened, but also *got* her—

Someone pulled up a chair right next to me: Gemma. I inhaled her powder smell as I glimpsed the pink streak in her hair again, which, up close, I could see was just a clip-on.

"Hullo," she said. "So listen to *this*: My dance partner has just now *completely* denied slipping me the love-poem-y thing."

"He has?"

"He has."

My heart sped.

She poked my arm. "Ace costume, Darth Vader."

I took off the cape. "It's not my Vader cape. It's my Cloak of Visibility."

She laughed. "Why, so it is. I remember it well. And what a gorgeous dress."

"You like it?" I stood up and twirled.

"It's amazing! I wish I had one half as pretty. Where did you get it?"

"A shop—spelled *s-h-o-p-p-e*—in Mantua that my big sister took me to last weekend. Maybe we'll take you sometime."

"Oh yes, I'd love that."

Mattie, you can't let your life be run by jerks.

"It's a date," I said.

Something crossed Gemma's face. A tiny eclipse.

Actually, um . . .

I panicked.

"Or we could go, and not call it a date," I added quickly.

"Or we could," Gemma said.

"Really? We don't have to—"

"No, I'd like to try it. *We* could try it."

She'd said we *again!*

"Let's just call it a 'dang,'" I said, fluttering my napkin. "What's in a name? That which we call a rose—"

"By any other name would smell as sweet," we finished together. Then we laughed. Loudly. A little awkwardly.

Not knowing what else to do then, I stared at the dance floor. "You looked like you were having fun with Liam," I said.

"Yes, I was. He's lovely. He says he thinks you're very

smart." She put her hand on my arm. "You should come dance with us."

"With you?" I looked into her eyes for a clue. "I mean, with you both?"

"With everyone," she said. "We're not paired up, really."

I saw she was right. Tessa was dancing with Liam now, Lucy was with Ajay and Isabel, and Keisha was with Willow and Jake and Charlotte. And so on. Just a big, messy bunch of eighth graders celebrating. Together.

"All right, I will," I said. I peeked at Mom, who was pouring some red juice into a punch bowl.

Gemma was smiling at me mischievously. "But can I tell you something first?"

"Sure."

"It's something I've wanted to say for a long time. And it's from my heart."

"Okay," I said, barely breathing.

She clutched her chest. "Matilda Monaghan," Gemma said in a fluttery, actressy voice, "thanks for being my one true Romeo."

"Thanks for being my *this*," I said, handing her the heart-shaped paper napkin smeared with potato chip grease.

She kissed my cheek, and then, laughing, pulled me onto the dance floor.

Tessa's Shakespearean Insults

p. 9: "like a toad; ugly and venomous"—*As You Like It*, II.i.13

p. 9: "[Whose] face is not worth sunburning"—*Henry V*, V.ii.147

p. 10: "Thou hast no more brain than I have in mine elbows."—*Troilus and Cressida*, II.i.44

p. 10: "I do wish thou wert a dog, that I might love thee something."—*Timon of Athens*, IV.iii.55–6

p. 13: "I'll beat thee, but I should infect my hands."—*Timon of Athens*, IV.iii.364

p. 13: "Vile worm, thou wast o'erlook'd even in thy birth."—*The Merry Wives of Windsor*, V.v.83

p. 13: "mad mustachio purple-hued malt-worm"—*Henry IV, Part 1*, II.i.75

p. 47: "canker blossom"—*A Midsummer Night's Dream*, III.ii.282

p. 84: "puke-stocking"—*Henry IV, Part 1*, II.iv.70

p. 84: "mildewed ear"—*Hamlet*, III.iv.64

p. 96: "carcass fit for hounds"—*Julius Caesar*, II.1.174

p. 198: "rat-catcher"—*Romeo and Juliet*, III.i.75

p. 199: "foul undigested lump"—*Henry VI, Part 2*, V.i.157

p. 199: "Thy head is as full of quarrels as an egg is full of meat."—*Romeo and Juliet*, III.1.23–4

p. 200: "Were I like thee, I'd throw away myself."—*Timon of Athens*, IV.iii.219

p. 201: "herd of boils and plagues"—*Coriolanus*, I.iv.31

p. 236: "false caterpillars"—*Henry VI, Part 2*, IV.iv.37

p. 236: "scurvy knaves"—*Romeo and Juliet*, II.iv.153, 162

p. 260: "monstrous malefactor"—*Antony and Cleopatra*, II.v.53

Acknowledgments

I'm happy that we live in an age when an author can suggest a book like *Star-Crossed*, and get the warmest possible support from her publisher. Loud cheers for my terrific editor, Alyson Heller, and for Fiona Simpson and Mara Anastas. A fancy bow for Margaret Kimball's gorgeous new illustrations, and for Nina Simoneaux for overseeing the new design in paperback.

A bouquet of roses for my superlative agent, Jill Grinberg, whose unflagging enthusiasm for this book made it possible. Hats off to Katelyn Detweiler, Cheryl Pientka, and Denise St. Pierre for all of their nurturing and expertise.

Blown kisses to those who read and commented on earlier drafts: Sarah Weston, Robynne Yokota, Michelle Pena. Violet Beller, you're my dream reader. I wish every author were lucky enough to have a Violet!

Group hug for my wonderful (and patient) family: Chris, Josh, Lizzy, Alex and Dani, Mom. Extra special thanks to Lizzy, for always brilliant editorial feedback and support, and to my husband, Chris, for being there for me in every word.

It's insane to give a shout-out to William Shakespeare, but I'd never forgive myself if I didn't. So to the Bard of Avon: Um, thanks. *R&J* is a really, really, REALLY good play.

Enjoy a sneak peek of

Everything I Know About You

Boxes

WE GOT TO SCHOOL IN the dark that morning, already fifteen minutes late.

By then, cars were headed in the opposite direction, doggy heads hanging out the passenger windows, horns honking good-bye. Ms. Jordan was standing by the fancy bus, wearing jeans (*she owned jeans?*), checking her clipboard. She looked up; now I could see she was talking to Ava Seeley and her mom, a blond woman dressed head to toe in beige, like she was about to go on a safari.

Suddenly I had the feeling Ava was glaring at me. I mean,

my brain told me she wasn't; we were maybe thirty feet away from her, in a car, and probably she couldn't even see me through the windshield. But she was the head clonegirl of our grade, basically my enemy, so I was always on the lookout for her nasty expressions.

"Gug," I said, my stomach knotting.

"Tally, don't *decide* this will be bad before anything happens," Mom said.

"Yeah, well. Too late."

"Come on, honey, you got this." Mom gave me a pep smile, which usually worked. Although not this time. "Just share the goodies Dad baked you; that'll help with the bus trip. Oh, and here's a present from me."

She handed me a small sandwich bag. Inside were two red things that looked like cap erasers.

"Earplugs," Mom explained. "For the bus. And the room, if Ava's a snorer."

"If she is, she couldn't be louder than Spike." My dog was a champion loud breather, so I was an expert at ignoring snores. Obviously, Mom meant the earplugs for more than snoring.

I stuck the bag in my pants pocket and threw my arms around her. "Thanks, Mom."

She smooched my cheek. "You're welcome, Daughter. Text me when you get there, okay? Tell Spider to text his mom too. And let me help with the bakery boxes."

We stepped out of the car into the sharp, chilly air. It didn't even feel like September, really—although maybe that was because it still seemed liked night. Maybe once we were on the road, and the sun was up, it would feel like a normal fall morning in Eastview.

But not yet. I shivered.

Mom carried two of the boxes, and I carried one, plus my duffel bag. The bus had this huge underneath storage compartment, but by now it was completely crammed with everyone's stuff for the next three days. So we had to wedge my duffel in sideways, probably squishing all the extra cookies Dad had packed.

Then we walked over to Ms. Jordan.

"Good morning, Tally!" Ms. Jordan greeted me too energetically, as if she'd had an extra cup of coffee for breakfast. "I was starting to worry you wouldn't make it. You're Mrs. Martin?" she asked Mom.

Mom caught my eye. Because I'm so much bigger and taller than the rest of my family, people say stuff like this sometimes. Maybe Ms. Jordan didn't mean it as an actual question—*Are you really Tally's mom?*—but it was hard to tell.

"Yes, I am," Mom said, smiling at everyone. Even at Ava, who didn't bother to smile back.

Although Ms. Jordan did. "Quite a daughter you have there. Full of character."

Mom nodded. You could tell she was trying to figure out if that was a compliment.

Meanwhile, Ava's mom was reaching out her hand to shake Mom's, completely ignoring the fact that Mom was holding two bulging bakery boxes. "Good morning. I'm Ellen Seeley," she announced. "I'm the parent chaperone for this trip."

The parent chaperone? But there were three other parents going, I was sure of it.

"Oh yes," Mom said pleasantly. "We've already met, Ellen. How nice of you to volunteer! Tally, could I please give you these boxes? The car is in a no-parking zone, so I really can't stay." Her eyes were begging; she obviously wanted to escape Ellen Seeley.

"Sure," I said, stacking Mom's boxes on top of mine. "You'd better hurry, so you don't get a ticket."

Mom tiptoed to kiss my cheek. "Have fun, sweetheart,

and remember those earplugs," she murmured. "Tune out *whatever* you need to, okay? And don't forget to text." Then she raced off.

Mrs. Seeley turned to talk to Ms. Jordan, as Ava narrowed her eyes at me. "So what's in the boxes?" Ava asked.

"Oh, these? Binoculars. Pickaxes. Flashlights. You know, assorted extremely high-tech devices for exploring our nation's capital."

"Huh," Ava said. She never appreciated my sense of humor. "It looks like bakery stuff."

"We're allowed to bring snacks," I informed her. "Not that I *am*."

"Whatever."

"What does *that* mean?"

"It means bring whatever you want, Tally. However *much* you want. I really don't care *what* you do, all right?"

"That's so funny, Ava," I replied. "Because you always act like exactly the opposite."

Now Ava definitely was glaring, and I glared right back at her. She was teeny, maybe ten inches shorter than me, so I had to stoop a bit to make eye contact. But it's hard to stoop while balancing three bakery boxes, so I sort of teetered in her direction.

Finally she said, "Well, you'd better get a seat. You're late, and we're about to leave."

And we know you'd hate to leave me behind, wouldn't you, Ava?

I climbed on board, my heart banging so loudly I was sure you could hear it over the bus engine.

Because here it was. We'd now arrived at the moment I'd been dreading for the past two weeks.

The moment I'd find out if my friends had shown up.

Or if I'd have to do this thing—all three days and four nights—stuck in a room alone with Ava Seeley.

We Hold These Truths

I STOOD AT THE FRONT of the crowded bus, balancing the boxes, scanning the rows. Where were they? Had Sonnet and Spider chickened out, the way I was terrified they would? Especially Spider, who'd texted me at eleven last night: Umm, not so sure about this. . . .

Nono, it will be fun!!!! I'd texted back.

But he'd never answered, which meant I hadn't slept very much, even with Spike's cuddling.

I looked past all the clonegirls in the front rows, then Mr. Gianelli and the chaperones: Mia Gilroy's mom, Althea

Packer's mom, Jamal Melton's dad. Finally I spotted Sonnet waving at me from the second-to-last row.

I breathed.

Then, clutching the boxes with sweaty hands, I made my way down the aisle, past classmates who were either half-asleep or much too perky for five fifteen in the morning.

The way this sort of fancy bus worked was window, two seats together, aisle, one seat, window. I guess to save the entire row, Sonnet and Spider had split up, with Sonnet sitting by the window in the two-seat part, and Spider across the aisle by himself. So, like usual, my seat was in the middle—next to Sonnet, across the aisle from Spider.

But also right in front of Marco Sarris and Trey Donaldson. Which meant that for the next six and one-quarter hours, there'd be no vacation from Spider's possibly former but I wasn't sure about this enemies.

Oh, bleep.

"Where *were* you, Tally?" Spider was asking. "Why were you late?" His soft brown eyes were enormous.

"Sorry," I said, handing him the top box. "Dad insisted on making cinnamon buns this morning. And then of course he had to do the icing. You didn't think I'd just forget to *show*, did you?"

I recycled Mom's pep smile for him, but he didn't smile back.

"Nah, I knew you'd make it," Spider admitted. He opened the box. "Whoa, awesome. Your dad rules."

"He definitely does," I said, giving the second box to Sonnet. "These are from the bakery. He made them yesterday, but they're still pretty fresh."

She squealed when she saw the box had giant chocolate chip cookies. My box had some Cinna-mmm muffins and a few blondies. To be honest, the cookies and blondies kind of made me queasy this hour of the morning, but I figured I'd change my mind about them later.

"We can trade," I announced as I settled into my seat. "Plus there's a ton more stuff in my duffel bag. Dad kind of went crazy with the bakery products. I barely had room for my treasure box."

"Wait," Sonnet said. "You brought your treasure box, Tally?" She asked this quietly, like it was a secret between the two of us.

"Yeah, of course. I'd never travel without my treasures. Why would I?"

"I don't know. Ms. Jordan said not to bring precious things on the trip, right?"

"Well, but they're not 'precious things.' Just precious to *me*."

"But what if they get lost or something?"

"That's why I brought the treasure box. So they *won't* get lost."

"I know, but." Sonnet began chewing on her thumbnail. "Maybe they're too precious for this trip."

Sonnet always dressed in such a careful, boring way—all her tops the colors of fall fruit, little gold studs in her ears, nothing in her straight black hair but a red ponytail holder—so probably she didn't understand why I needed my treasures with me. But I knew she thought they were cool, because she said so all the time. She even used that specific word: "cool."

Was Sonnet worried that they wouldn't be safe in a room with Ava? Or was she worried about something else? Either way, it was extremely strange.

I glanced over at Spider. He was fine, just eating a bun and reading one of his space books. I didn't envy a whole lot about him, but his ability to read wherever—in moving vehicles, the noisy cafeteria, dark movie theaters—seemed kind of like a superpower, really. And he didn't even need earplugs.

A jab on my shoulder.

"Hey, Math Girl, your dad *baked* you all of that?" Marco was practically hanging over my seat, salivating like a cartoon wolf.

"Yeah," I said. "He's a baker. So you know, he bakes."

"Cool. You're so lucky."

"Yeah, I know."

"Wish someone in *my* family baked like that."

Obviously, he was waiting for me to offer him something. Well, too bad for him. I didn't forget things so easily. And I didn't feel the need to bribe him. At least, not yet.

Sonnet's cheeks were already bulging with cookie. "Eelikeshoo," she murmured.

"What?"

She chewed and swallowed. Then she leaned over and whispered with chocolate breath: "He likes you."

Check out the stories you love with a brand-new look!